RCML2
JF
10.99

D0069480

Spring Frost

Bitter Frost #7

of Kailin Gow's Frost Series

RALEIGH COUNTY PUBLIC LIBRARY
221 N. KANAWHA ST.
BECKLEY, WV 25801

kailin gow

Spring Frost: Frost #7

Spring Frost (Frost Series #7)
Published by THE EDGE
THE EDGE is an imprint of Sparklesoup Inc.
Copyright © 2012 Kailin Gow

All Rights Reserved. No part of this book may be reproduced or transmitted in any form or by any means, graphic, electronic, or mechanical, including photocopying, recording, taping or by any information storage or retrieval system, without the permission in writing from the publisher except in case of brief quotations embodied in critical articles and reviews. Do NOT post on websites or share this book without permission from copyright holder. We take piracy seriously.

All characters and storyline is an invention from Kailin Gow. Any resemblance to people alive or dead is purely coincidence.

For information, please contact:

THE EDGE at Sparklesoup
14252 Culver Dr., A732
Irvine, CA 92604
www.sparklesoup.com
First Edition.
ISBN 13: 978-1-59748-036-9

DEDICATION

To all who believe in the healing power of love.

Prologue

I remembered Clariss well. I had spent many childhood afternoons with tears streaming down my grubby cheeks, hiding in the woods behind Gregory High, willing the pain to go away. Even after all the horrors I had seen in Feyland – death, destruction, war, chaos – there was something about her cold green eyes that sent a shiver down my spine. I remembered how she used to treat me in the old days – she would toss her long, glossy golden hair over her smooth and milky-white shoulder, raise a perfectly plucked eyebrow and look at me with savage contempt. Clariss had made my life a living hell. Before there was Feyland, before there was the escape that Kian offered me, there were days of dreading going to school, days of avoiding her in the locker room or in the hall, trying to escape from her endless reign of cruelty. Clariss wasn't an ordinary "popular girl" – she wasn't mean because she was insecure or thoughtless because she hadn't grown up yet, or imitating an overly-obnoxious mother, or any one of the solutions my mother had proposed to me when trying to cheer me up about Clariss' behavior. "She's probably just lonely," my mother had said, smoothing my hair, "and she doesn't know how to express her feelings. Don't be afraid of her, be sorry for her. She doesn't know how to love – and so she's probably suffering far worse than you are right now." But I knew better. My mother, with her optimistic view of things and need to see the best in people, wanted to believe that Clariss was a lost soul in need of comfort and guidance, a young and troubled girl who would, with any luck, grow up one day to be a perfectly decent human being. I knew better. Clariss wasn't motivated by fear or loneliness or insecurity or anything at all. She was motivated by pure evil. She wanted to see those around her suffering; she relished the sweetness of tears. Even when we were young children, Clariss always liked to push us to the ground, cackling over our scraped knees and bruised thighs. She fed off other people's unhappiness; she relished our suffering. Her other minions – girls like Lauren and Kate – were merely insecure, tittering because they felt like they had to in order to avoid having that same terrifying wrath turned back on them, to avoid being the objects of her scorn. But not Clariss. Clariss just wanted to watch as she sent a girl sobbing to the bathroom, as she convinced a heavier girl that bulimia was "the only solution" to her social woes, as she tore an unfashionable scarf off a girl's neck and ripped it to shreds in the hallway.

Clariss always got whatever she wanted. She had a power of glamoring stronger than any I had seen among the Fey: she could come across like the manifestation of pure evil when she was alone with me, but the second a teacher walked into the room, she had the power to convince him that she was all sweetness and light. She would bat her long lashes and turn her emerald-green gaze upon him and shake her long blond hair; false tears would appear like diamonds at the corner of her eye and she would complain bitterly about how I – or anyone else she'd been bullying – had in fact been grievously abusing HER.

The teachers fell for it. Every single time. I can't even remember how many times I took the fall for Clariss' cruelty, how many hours I spent in detention being ordered to "think about what you've done" while Clariss got off scot-free, glaring at me with a cruel and glimmering smile from the corridor while I sat hunched over my desk, composing an essay on why "bullying is bad."

So perhaps I shouldn't have been surprised to discover that Clariss was, after all, a creature of magic like me. I'd suspected it often enough at school – how many times had Logan and I sighed together that "she's not really human – she can't be?" How many times had I bitterly complained "she must be some kind of monster? How else could she be casting a spell on all those teachers like that?" But now, as I stared at the beautiful, motionless face of Clariss before me, its implacable glare at once alluring and terrifying, I realized that I had been right all along.

Spring Frost: Frost #7

All my childhood fears, all my insecurities – they hadn't been paranoid at all! Just as I had always known, always sensed, that there was something different about me, so too had I always known deep down that there had always been something truly evil about Clariss.

No, I thought to myself. Not always. There had been a time when Clariss seemed kind to me. A picture began forming in my mind – a fuzzy image, out of focus. A sandbox. Spring. Birds chirping old songs and the fragrance of honeysuckle in the bushes. Two girls sitting together, playing with dolls. One with beautiful golden hair; one with caramel-colored braids. Me and Clariss. We had been friends once, hadn't we? I thought back, trying harder to remember. Hadn't we? Perhaps not good friends, but she had been nice enough to me, to everybody. None of us thought of her as a "bully."

And then we must have been six or seven – I remembered that we were bigger, the sandbox was smaller. I remembered the three of us sitting in the sandbox: me, Logan, and Clariss. I remembered how happy I had been on that day – Logan and I had plans to go to the woods and go exploring for dinosaur footprints, which Patrick McGuire swore existed deep within the sylvan depths of the forest.

"We're going to find a brontosaurus," Logan was saying cheerfully, "and a Tyrannosaurus Rex, and a stegosaurus, and maybe even a mastodon!"

"I don't think there are dinosaur bones in the forest," Clariss was saying, re-applying her lip gloss. Even at six Clariss was well-aware of the need to be fashionable.

"What about you, Bree?" Logan turned to me with an excited, expectant look on his face. "You'll come, right? We'll go see the dinosaurs.'"

"Of course!" I sprang to my feet. "My mom says she'll stand behind a tree so we can pretend she's not there and that we're exploring. I want to see the dinosaur bones. I bet we'll find a big skull with lots of sharp teeth and then we can make the teeth into weapons like the ones the knights used and chase people with them!"

Clariss' smile froze on her lips.

"Gosh, Bree," Logan laughed. "You're the best girl ever, did you know that? I used to think my cousin Jamie was the best girl in the world but now I think it's you."

I caught a glimpse of Clariss' face at that moment. Its pert, innocent beauty had been transformed – for a second – by ugliness. A look of black hate appeared in her eyes; her jaw hardened and her mouth soured. She glared at me with blazing fire in her gaze.

"What is it, Clariss?" Logan turned to Clariss in confusion. "Is everything okay?"

Clariss did not respond, instead fixing her look of hate straight on me. Without saying a word, she rose to her feet, staring me down. "There!" she cried at last, pushing me down into the sand. "You're so stupid, Breena. You think you're all cool because you can find dinosaurs, but you're just too stupid to know that you won't find any. Logan's only taking you to the woods because he feels sorry for you because you're ugly and nobody else likes you. And nobody else ever will!"

Logan and I looked on in shock as Clariss stormed off. "What was that about?" Logan asked me.

I shrugged.

But from that day forth, a new and furious power had taken hold of Clariss. She no longer played with us – she no longer even came near us, unless it was to torment me or insult me. She began insulting the other children, too, mocking this one's clothing or that one's hair, this one's weight or that one's parents' divorce. Nothing was off-limits; nothing was sacred. Clariss' cruelty extended to anything and everything.

Except for Logan. Logan was the one exception to Clariss' reign of terror. She never insulted him; she was never mean to him. When she grew older and began discarding boys two or three at a time, laughing when she ripped up their roses or stomped on their chocolates, Logan was somehow immune to her callous cruelty. He refused to participate when she persuaded the rest of the class to march in a circle around me, shouting insults and pointing fingers and telling me I was a "bastard" because my mother didn't know who my father was. He told her off when she mocked the dresses my mother had painstakingly made. He refused all her myriad invitations to sit with her and her minions at lunch, saying only "If Breena's not welcome here, than I'm not either."

If Logan had intended to force Clariss' hand, to pressure her into being nice to me, then he had failed magnificently. The more Logan stood up for me, the more Logan took my side, the meaner Clariss was to me. The more Logan refused her increasingly obvious advances, the more she took out her frustration on me. Logan was the only man she couldn't get, we both knew, and that was – in Clariss' twisted, petty mind – my fault. And this meant that I had to be punished.

Things only got worse when we hit high school. As Clariss' crush on Logan intensified, so did her attacks on me. The few female friends I had in junior high crept away, one by one, to join Clariss' gang, figuring that her sometime cruelty to them was vastly preferably to what they would have gone through if she had associated them with me. I stopped getting invited to birthday parties; I started eating lunch alone. Only Logan stood by me through it all, unconvinced by Clariss' increasingly desperate attempts to lure him into her circle of friends.

"Even if she weren't mean to you personally," Logan said, "I wouldn't hang out with her. She's a bully, through and through; she's just looking to control the people around her. She doesn't even have a crush on me – not really – she's just upset that she can't have whatever she wants, when she wants it. And the fact that she's horrible to you – well, let's just say that if she's looking for a way into my heart, she's not about to find it by hurting one of my best friends. She thinks she can pressure me into hating you, but it's not going to work, Bree. I'm never going to leave your side. Best friends, remember?"

Yet despite Logan's strength – and my mother's unending encouragement – high school was still a daily eight hours of torment for me. Clariss soon decided sabotaging my friendships wasn't enough – she started sabotaging my other passions, intentionally destroying the posters I carefully put up all over school for the "Environmental Protection Club" and defacing my "Save the Woods" banner that Logan and I had spent all night working on.

It was no surprise, in retrospect, that it was Clariss' mother – a wealthy industrialist – who spearheaded the movement to knock down Gregory's woods and build a strip mall there instead. Clariss' parents, powerful though they were, were helpless when it came to combating her tantrums. They did whatever she wanted. And what she wanted was to destroy me.

Chapter 1

I looked over at Clariss' cold, proud face. She had aged – I noticed that right away. I remembered her as a lithe, lovely girl of sixteen, her haughty imperiousness still budding; her legs growing longer, her skirt growing ever shorter. But the woman I saw before me was no adolescent girl. She was an adult. She was a young adult in her early 20s.

For an instant, I was shocked. *What had happened to Clariss?* But then it hit me. Clariss had gotten older – just as I had. Time in Feyland often seemed so strange and moribund: with the twin suns of Feyland gone, we hadn't been able to tell one day from another. But at least two must have gone by since I had first entered Feyland, first gone Beyond the Crystal River. But Clariss looked even older than that – she must have been twenty-three or older. I remembered what Kian had told me – "time in Feyland works differently than time in the mortal world." Only a few years had gone by in Feyland – but back in the mortal world, time must have rushed by. The people I knew in high school would likely have grown up, graduated, gotten jobs, married. And as I looked down into Clariss' face, the full force of those years struck me.

I wasn't a kid anymore. I wasn't a child, easily reduced to tears by Clariss' adolescent jests. This was something bigger than that. A cheerleader's torments couldn't' frighten me any longer. I had grown past those days – forgotten Clariss and the cruelty she inflicted on me. I had bigger problems to worry about. But Clariss hadn't changed. She had gotten older, to be sure – her girlish charms had vanished and a more womanly beauty had taken their place. But in her eyes I could detect the same jealous glare, the same malicious glint in her gaze. Nothing had changed for Clariss – that much was clear. She still hated me as much as ever. She still looked at me with disdain so powerful it could have shrivelled up the grass on the plains of Feyland.

No, nothing had changed for Clariss – until this moment. Until now.

"Who would have thought..." Clariss was smiling wickedly, "that it would end up like this, eh Treena? Who would have thought that we'd meet again like this?"

Had the Sorceress possessed Clariss? I turned to Kian and Logan, who were staring at Clariss with shock on their faces. I gritted my teeth. I may not have liked Clariss, but if she had been possessed by the sorceress, she was probably in as much danger as I was.

"Listen, Clariss..." words failed me. I looked up in confusion. What was Clariss even *doing* here? It wasn't safe for a mortal like her – I knew that much. "Clariss, do you even know where you are? Are you okay?" My voice was slow, full of trepidation, as if I were calling to a kitten up a tree.

"Oh, for Christ's sake, Treena, of course I know where I am." Clariss gave a snort. "A place only someone like you would dare to dream up, I'm sure. Feyland." She scoffed. "I should have figured it out years ago – that you were one of them. It was so obvious, in retrospect. I knew there was some reason I hated you."

Logan cleared his throat loudly, stepping forward. His broad shoulders stood squarely between me and Clariss. His face was filled with shock. "Clariss – do you know who *you* are?" He turned back towards me. "The Sorceress might not have taken over – she might have some part of her..."

"I know who I am!" snapped Clariss. "Clariss Dickens."

Logan's voice was soft and gentle – even caressing. Something about his calm, familiar voice made the tension in my stomach dissipate. "Then you know you don't want to be here, Clariss. You know this isn't the place for you. You've got to fight whatever it is that's controlling you, Clariss. You have to fight it."

"Oh, Logan," Clariss rolled her eyes. "Logan, Logan, Logan. You're always so noble – always so chivalrous. You always were so blind – you only ever had eyes for that ridiculous, gangly, skinny..." she didn't even bother to identify me by name. "Haven't you figured it out, Logan? I *do* want to be here. I want *here.*" She looked around over the horizon of

Feyland. "I want *this.*" Her eyes shone with anger and terrifying power.

"This?"

"Feyland," spat Clariss through gritted teeth. "All of it. The power. The rivers. The mountains. The forests. Winter and Summer. It's mine."

Logan looked concerned. "You can't possibly want this, Clariss," he said, reaching out to her. "It isn't yours. It isn't anybody's. It doesn't belong to you – but rather to the people of Feyland."

Clariss gave a seductive pout, her dark eyes fixating on Logan's face. "And is that what you say to Treena when she plays Queen over this whole realm? Do you tell *her* to stop playing her fairy-tale games?"

"It's Breena, actually," I was trying to keep my cool. I wasn't going to let my high school bully get between me and my kingdom. But I couldn't deny that Clariss' words needled in my heart, bringing back memories of the pain I had faced. "And you are in my kingdom now, Clariss. I recommend you go back where you came from – and quickly, too. You don't want to cause trouble here, Clariss. Not in my place. Keep Gregory for yourself and your family.

Build whatever strip malls you please. But you are not welcome here."

We were interrupted by the sound of hoof-beats. The knights were riding down, one by one, from the perilous cliff top, from which the suns were now gradually emerging. Each one had his lance in the air, his sword pointed squarely at Clariss. They knew what I knew – even without recognizing her. Clariss was an enemy, through and through.

"Surround her!" I heard myself ordering. Instantly the knights made a ring around Clariss, the points of their swords gleaming in the newly raised sunlight.

Clariss looked up at me with an arched eyebrow, her expression mocking and cold. "Really Breena," she said, faintly pretending to be shocked. "Is that how you choose to greet an old friend?"

Images of our shared past were rushing through my brain – Clariss laughing at me, her taunts and remarks, rumors spread in the lunchroom, rude words written on my locker, a gaze colder than ice, my friends leaving me, one by one...I had forgotten how painful those memories were; all at once, they hit me with a full force and sent me reeling. Memories of pain; memories of anger. Memories of a time before I knew who I was, or why I was special.

Memories of a time when I was a nobody.

I shook my head, willing the bad thoughts to fly out of my brain. "Funny," I said, doing my best to keep my voice steady. "I don't remember ever being friends with you."

"Good..." Clariss' smile broadened, the ends of her mouth twisting maliciously. "I'm glad." Clariss took a step forward, looking me up and down. "That means I won't have any regrets."

"About what?" Logan turned around threateningly.

"This!"

In an instant, Clariss had darted forward; I saw the glint of a knife shining before me, and then I saw nothing but darkness. I could only feel a pain hotter than fire, colder than ice, like acid in my veins. I could hear myself cry out in pain; I could feel the blood pouring from my stomach. I doubled forward, falling to my knees. My head was heavy all of a sudden – so heavy....Clariss' triumphant face glimmered in and out of focus as I felt my head loll forward, the crown I wore falling to the earth.

"There..." Clariss was kneeling before me, her hands scraping at the earth as she picked up the crown and put it upon her own head. "See. Let's see who is Queen of Feyland now – how about that, eh?"

"Breena!" I could hear Kian's voice – shocked and filled with pain. I could feel his agony – our telepathic connection stronger than ever. *Please Breena*, he seemed to be saying as he enveloped me in his arms. *Please, Breena, hold on – be strong – please, Breena, stay with me.*

"Clariss?" I muttered sleepily.

"How dare you!" Logan had rushed forward, roaring with anger as he lunged at Clariss, sword in hand. I could see the despair on his face as he slashed his sword into empty air: Clariss had turned into a pillar of dark smoke before our eyes, vanishing as quickly as she had appeared into nothingness.

"No!" roared Logan. He turned to me and I could see, through vision that grew increasingly fuzzy, the hollow emptiness of his eyes. "Breena, hold on!"

"Breena!" It was Kian's voice – and Logan's – mingling with the cries of others....Shasta, Rodney, Alistair, Rose...

"Hold on, please hold on..."

But their voices were only echoes. I could hear nothing more.

Chapter 2

Suddenly, it was as if I had been split in two. My body remained upon the earth, blood – silver, now – pouring out from my inert body. But I wasn't part of that body. I felt as if I were floating above the scene – watching from a distance. Unable to speak. Unable to move. Unable to cry out. All I could do was watch what was happening to me – take in the sight of my splayed-out body, sickening in its misshapen pose – and try in vain to stem my terror.

"Breena!" Kian was crying out, falling to his knees beside me. "Please, Breena – I'm so sorry. So sorry..." Silver tears were falling upon his snow-white cheeks. His customary marble hardness was gone – now he looked open. Vulnerable. I ached to comfort him, to wrap my arms around him and tell him that everything would be all right. But I couldn't move. I felt at once lighter than air and heavier than lead, unable to do anything but watch. "I'm so sorry, Kian..." I tried to speak, but I could say nothing.

"What are you waiting for?" Logan was shouting. "Heal her – heal her now!" He shoved Kian in the direction of my body.

"I *am* trying – leave me alone! Leave me alone!" Now Kian was shouting too, his voice booming and echoing throughout the mountain peaks. He placed his hands upon my wound, and I watched as silver and blue light appeared around his fingers. He closed his eyes, concentrating harder, pressing the light to my wounds.

But nothing happened. The wound continued to gush blood; the light died from Kian's fingers.

"What's going on?" Logan crouched down beside Kian. "Why isn't it working? She's not healing! What's happening?" He too was stifling back sobs. My heart ached for both of them – for the two men I had loved. For the two men who shared my heart – both of whom would always have it. Only minutes ago we had been fighting – only minutes ago, I had been angry with both of them; they had both been angry with each other. But now Kian and Logan were each trying to hold my hand, grieving side by side, their rivalry forgotten. They remembered only love.

"She's been poisoned," Rose said in a small voice. "I think that's what's happened. The magic in that dagger – it was strong magic, the kind that can instantly kill fey. It's not just the wound that's the problem. Poisonous dark magic has made its way into her body – you can see here, her blood's turning black."

"By the sword of Calthon!" Kian buried his face in his hands. "Is there nothing we can do? Can't you heal her?"

Rose looked uncertain. "I'll try," she said, color spreading to her cheeks. "But I don't know what good it will do. When a poison as powerful as this one is dealt out, often the only antidote can come from the source."

"You mean the Sorceress?" Logan said darkly. "I should have slain her on the spot – I should have known…I shouldn't have tried to save Clariss, should have never given her the chance…"

"It's not your fault." Kian's words were hollow, empty. "You couldn't have known. None of us could have known." He looked up at Rose with black eyes smeared with crying. "Can we stop it from getting worse, Rose? Even if we can't heal her altogether – is there any way we can contain the damage?" He sighed heavily as he turned to Logan. "Logan, my Winter magic is failing me. Is there nothing you or your kind can do?"

"No!" Logan almost spat. "No – we Wolf Fey have no magic at all." He bit his lip. "And I have never been more bitterly ashamed of that than at this moment – when I would give everything I have to be able to heal her."

"Kian!" I wanted to call out. "Don't use your Winter magic – use our combine magic! Maybe that will....only that will..." I closed my eyes. Wherever I was – stuck between life and death – I had to make it back into my own body. I had to will myself to stay alive moments longer. A strange, calm feeling had come over me – as if I had been drugged. A part of me wanted to float off, to float away from this scene: from the stress, from the pain. Just leave my body behind and float to wherever Feyland was calling me next. How easy it would have been, I felt – just to let myself float away...

But then I caught sight of Kian's face. Of his tears, which watered the earth. Of the silver streaks upon his face. No – I couldn't leave him. I couldn't leave my love behind. I had to fight it; I had to fight this feeling. I had to stay strong, to stay alive, to get back into my own body. I closed my eyes, concentrating every force of my being, trying to find the power within me: the orange flames of Summer, the heat that was the source of my power.

I felt something rip within my soul – a great tearing power that coursed through me all at once, obliterating everything else.

Suddenly my eyes shot open. "Kian!" I started.

"Breena – you're conscious!"

I was in my own body again. My own heavy, earthly body. Able to speak. Able to look into Kian's beautiful blue eyes....

"Kian, I'm so sorry...I love you so much...."

"Stay with me, Breena!" He held my hand to his chest; Logan was holding my other hand to his lips.

Spring Frost: Frost #7

"Our combined power…" I whispered. "Summer and Winter together." I winced in pain; I could feel the knife-wound now more profoundly than before. I could feel the poison burning my blood from the inside out. "Try again, Kian, I'll try too."

Kian's hands worked their way up and down my body, trying desperately to restore circulation to me. Blue flames appeared again at his fingertips. I closed my eyes, willing my own orange fire to appear.

"Try harder, Breena!" Logan was saying. "Try to live – want to live…"

Somewhere, in the back of my mind, I heard a hazy voice, barely louder than an echo. The voices I had heard back in the Kingdom of the Dead: the Queens of Feyland.

"Now is not your time, Breena. Breena, you must be strong. Breena, you must survive. You must live – for Feyland. Be strong, Breena. Be true!"

I closed my eyes, willing my body to obey me. Trying to tap into the source of the powers of Feyland. *I will not be defeated*, I told myself. *Not by Clariss. Not by the Sorceress. Not by anyone else. Feyland needs me.* In the distance, I caught sight of the two suns of Feyland, rising slowly into the sky, spreading out their gorgeous sunbeams across the mountainside. *We saved Feyland once*, I thought to myself. *We must do it again. They need us. They will always need us.*

"Breena, please try!" Kian pressed his lips to mine. His touch warmed me; it electrified me. It gave me strength. Suddenly, slowly, orange flames began to appear at the edges of my body, circling around my wound. Fire began to surround him, too: the silvery arctic blue of the Winter Fey. And his fire melded with mine – orange and blue, gold and silver – until we could not distinguish our two flames, but instead burned only with a single bright passion. A single love.

I screamed with pain. I could feel the force of the magic rip through me like an earthquake. But I didn't let go of Kian's hand. I didn't turn my gaze from his.

The blue and orange flames seemed to cocoon me, to keep me safe. They began to soothe the pain in my stomach; the wound began to close, until all that was left was a single, jagged black scar. The bleeding had stopped. I looked down: there was color in my wrists again.

The glowing stopped, and I fell back into Kian's arms.

"Breena, are you okay?" Kian was covering my face with kisses, his joy feeding my own.

"Yeah – I think so. For now...."

I could see Logan standing a few feet away. I could see upon his face a mixture of joy and pain. Relief – that I was not dead. And agony – that his arms were not the ones I fell into, not the ones that cradled me as I returned to life. I saw Rose tiptoe to Logan's side, her face troubled, too. She put out a hand upon his arm; he jerked up in surprise.

"She's stable," Rose was saying, forcing out a smile. "Don't worry, Logan. We've slowed down the damage. Now we can focus on making her well." She brushed a stray hair out of Logan's eyes. "I'll do my best to heal her."

Logan nodded, wiping away his tears.

Rose knelt beside me. "I'm going to put you to sleep now, Breena. So we can start to work on healing you. Just rest, okay? Just relax."

I nodded, still exhausted.

Rose put her hands upon the black scar, white flames shooting from her fingertips. Neither cold nor hot, these flames were comforting. Pure. Around them the air smelled like jasmine and honeysuckle. I felt a reassuring sense of warmth – like hot cocoa – course through me. My muscles began to relax; I leaned my head in Kian's lap.

"Just close your eyes, Breena," Rose was saying.

I could have smiled to myself. Rose had become quite the alchemist, I thought to myself. I reminded myself to tell her so – but it was too late. Sleep had already wrapped its dark arms about me. I would tell her in the morning.

Chapter 3

I woke up the smell of baking bread. Its warm, slightly sweet aroma filled my nostrils, flooding my consciousness with light and heat. I could almost taste the savory crust on the tip of my tongue. My skin felt pleasantly warm, as if I had bathed in the hot springs of Winter Peak; the whole room was glowing. My eyes were closed, but I could sense the golden warmth of the room from behind my eyelids. My whole body ached, but it was a pleasant ache – a slow progress from exhaustion to energy. I opened my eyes slowly, stretching every inch of my body out upon the soft pillows. I looked around, hazy with confusion. This wasn't a place I recognized – I had never been here before. Golden fabric adorned the room; bright silk tapestries hung down from the beamed wooden ceilings. I recognized the stories depicted on them – tales of the great heroes and heroines of Feyland like the first Queen and Panthea and Calthon – tales that I had grown to devour during my time in Feyland. I traced the outline of each sumptuous form with my eyes, looking at the tapestries and taking in their beauty

"Breena?" The voice was soft and caressing. It was a light, lilting woman's voice. Immediately I turned my head in the direction of the sound.

"Oh, you're awake!" It was Rose, her long red hair plaited in braids upon her head. She had a cool compressing cloth in her hand, and was wearing the crisp white robes of the royal nurses. "Thank goodness – it's been long enough. I'll go notify King Kian right away – he's been so worried." She leaped to her feet, tossing back her violently red hair. She looked older, I thought. More womanly, somehow. I'd never noticed before that Rose was beautiful – to me, she'd always been younger, a child. But now she looked more confident, more self-assured. A certain grace shone through her every motion. I smiled to myself. Time really was going by quickly in Feyland – even little Rose was now a woman in her own right.

She turned to go, but I stopped her. My mind

was racing with unanswered questions. "Wait, Rose," I called. "Where are we? Where is everyone – what's going on? I don't know this place."

Rose's mouth widened in a kind and gentle smile. "No need to worry, my Queen. Everything is all right. We are safe here. We are in the castle of the Duke of Autumn Springs. He has placed us under his protection while you recover."

"Autumn Springs..." Where had I heard that name before? "Isn't that where Alistair's from? Is it Alistair's father we're staying with?" I thought back, but the memories were hazy. "I've heard tell of this great place."

"Not his father, my Queen, but rather his uncle. His father is the younger brother of the Duke, and died when Alistair was very young. Alistair is being raised to be the Duke's heir – and heir to the title. Of course, it's not the same as being a Duke anywhere else."

"Of course not." Autumn Springs, I knew, was technically independent from Feyland – it had been ever since the Wars of the Leaves two hundred years ago. Technically I had no sovereignty here – the highest rulers were the independent Dukes of Autumn Springs. They had more power than almost anyone else in Feyland. And – more importantly – they had been neutral in the wars between Winter and Summer, refusing to affiliate even with Autumn proper. As a result, they had become a prosperous center of trade as war refugees began to set up shop and start trading inside the boundaries of the Springs.

"We didn't want to spread word you were ill to your own kingdom," Rose said. "News might have gotten out – and enough people want your power that we didn't think it was a good idea to start bandying rumors about. So Alistair's uncle...."

"Is this where you met Alistair, then?" I asked. I watched with surprise how Rose's creamy cheeks turned blazing red. She blushed and did not meet my eyes. "No – no," she said, casting her eyes down to the floor. "This is actually my second time here in Autumn Springs. I've actually been here before when I visited Alistair after he left the Summer Kingdom because of this...incident...with the Pixies. But when I met Alistair, it wasn't here. It was in the Summer

Kingdom."

"You two seem to know each other awfully well," I said, unable to resist a smile as Rose awkwardly began patting my forehead with the cool cloth. "I was wondering why he doesn't seem to notice anyone else the second you walk into the room. I didn't realize you knew each other so well."

"Oh, not *very* well," said Rose, with a blush that belied her words. "We were young apprentices together in the Summer Court years and years ago. We worked together in order to study to be alchemists."

"I see," I said.

"You see what?" Rose looked startled – almost scared.

"You know each other very well then."

"Well, I wouldn't say...." Rose shuffled in place. "Yes, I suppose so."

"Come on, Rose..." There was something about her awkward innocence that reminded me of myself when I was her age – she was so young, so unsure. Just as I had been. She deserved the confidence that Feyland had given me. "It's okay to like him back, you know."

"What?" Rose looked shocked.

"It's okay to care for each other in that way. It's a good thing. There's no shame in that." But Rose looked too embarrassed, so I decided to change the topic. "Anyway, how is Alistair doing? I know he was stricken quite badly by the Book of the Dark Sorceress before – is he better now? Last I saw him all his strength had gone."

Rose sighed deeply. "My Queen," she began. "I am sorry to say that he has not fully recovered, although fortunately he is not as stricken as before. The Dark Sorceress's powers are strong. Even her book has powers of its own." I could see from Rose's worried face how much she cared for Alistair, and I felt ashamed of teasing her. If Alistair's life still hung in the balance, the last thing Rose needed was to worry about her own love for him. But as Rose's face darkened, another blush came over her cheek. She opened her mouth, as if to say something, but then rapidly closed it again.

"Rose?"

"Yes, my Queen?" She did not meet my eyes.

"Rose – is there something you're not telling me? About Alistair, I mean? I know you don't want to worry me, and that's very brave and noble of you, but I do want to help if I can. Because you can tell me anything, Rose. You don't have to worry about my feelings. It's important to tell me everything that has happened, if you can."

Rose swallowed hard, gulping. "Queen Breena," she began.

"Just Breena," I put out a hand onto her shoulder. "You're Rodney's sister, after all – and he's always called me just Breena. You've saved my life more than once; you've saved Logan's life. I think you deserve to call me by my first name. After all, without you, Feyland would still be in darkness."

Rose exhaled sharply. "Okay, Breena," she said. "It seems that...the magic of the book has some quite specific ill-effects. The Sorceress's magic doesn't kill all at once; rather it's a slow poison. And in Alistair's case, I fear the book has poisoned his mind. He seems fully recovered – at least, at first. But other times he seems...distracted. He forgets his words mid-sentence; I've heard him muttering to himself – or to invisible figures in the room. His eyes glaze over and I see such pain in them. I fear the book's influence is still upon him."

I nodded. "Very well," I said. "Thank you for telling me, Rose. Listen – our first priority is to ensure everyone's safety. We have to be careful to ensure that Alistair doesn't harm himself – or anyone around him. Maybe we should install a sentry outside his bedroom door."

"Yes, Qu...Breena." But Rose still looked uncomfortable – like there was something she was trying to keep from me.

"What is it, Rose?" I sat up in bed. "You still seem...is there anything else you're not telling me?"

"Like what?" Rose was a poor liar – I could see it in her eyes.

"You seem fully recovered, it is true. Like Alistair..." Rose faltered, and I saw where this was going.

"But I'm not?"

"I don't know. The Sorceress's magic powers are so very strong. And the poison in that dagger was intense. I'm afraid, Breena...I'm afraid the poison isn't done with you yet. It hasn't manifested itself yet, but it could..."

Rose turned around, and instantly I saw the glint of the knife in her hand. My heart started pounding as I leaped from my bed. Rose, too, under the influence of the Dark Sorceress? Little Rose? I couldn't believe it. I grabbed Rose and wrestled her to the floor; the knife dropped and slid across the stone floor. "Dark Sorceress!" I cried out, my voice full of rage, "you will not take her! Your quarrel is with me..."

"Breena!" Rose was calling in a small voice. "Breena, calm down!" She was pinned to the ground beneath me, shaking like a leaf in an autumn wind. "Breena, it's me, Rose. I'm not trying to hurt you."

I sat up, looking at her with shock. Rose was staring at me in terror. "I'm sorry; I didn't mean to scare you..."

"No, it's fine." Now it was my turn to blush. Why had I reacted so quickly with anger – reacted so violently? Rose didn't look injured, thank goodness, but she was certainly shaken. Her skin was chalk-white and she could not meet my eyes. "I just got spooked, after what happened to Alistair. Why did you have that knife?"

"I had to show you..." Rose said. "I needed to see..."

"See what?"

"The poison." Rose looked downcast. "I'm sorry, I should have warned you. But I was afraid." She slowly made her way towards the knife. "May I show you, Breena?"

"What do you need a knife to show me the poison for?"

"I'm so sorry, Breena." Rose's voice trembled. "I need you to give me the palm of your hand. It'll only be a little prick."

Rose and I stared at each other for a while. I hesitated, but the kind look in her eyes told me that she was telling the truth – the Dark Sorceress had no power over her. I held out my palm to hers. She picked up the knife gingerly and – with an apologetic look in her eyes – lightly pricked the skin at my palm.

I winced as a small wound opened up in my hand. But as I looked more closely at the injury, my pain turned to panic, to fear. The blood that dripped from my injury was no longer silver. Instead – streaming in rivulets down my wrist – it was a sickly, blue-tinted shade of green.

Chapter 4

❄

The whole room began to shake and shift. I put out a hand to steady myself, getting greenish blue blood on the creamy white bed sheets. My heart was beating so loud that I could barely hear Rose's cries of "Breena!" over the din. I could feel my whole body shaking with fear, shock, and confusion. The change in blood color could come from only one reason – a change in identity, a change in the most fundamental and basic level of magic. Humans had red blood; fairies had silver blood. The color of the blood was part of the deepest magical identity. And the only creatures I'd ever heard of who had green-blue blood were...

"Rose..." my voice was shaking so that I could barely speak. "Is it true? Am I....a pixie?"

Rose was silent for a while. "You don't look like a pixie, Breena," she said at last. "Your skin and features are unchanged; your ears aren't pointed. You don't have the appearance of a pixie."

"Nor the smell of one!" A kindly male voice broke the silence.

"Logan?"

I looked up and smiled with involuntary relief. "You knew?"

He sat down beside me, grinning at me as he took my hand. "Rose just told us she suspected – the blood on your clothes when you were wounded had gone a funny color...but don't worry. If you were a pixie I'd have smelled you from the corridor." The bags under Logan's eyes testified to many worried and sleepless nights, but somehow he still managed to look like the bright morning sun – radiant and energetic. His joy at my recovery was clear in his eyes – as he took my hand, I could feel the warmth of his skin coursing through me, comforting me. I was a little less frightened now.

Rose turned an even brighter shade of red; her face now resembled little so much as a tomato from the Summer Valley farms. "I've – uh – got to go get the King..." she stumbled over her words. "Make sure he knows she's awake...."

She nearly tripped over a bronze statue of Calthon as she exited the room. Logan took my hands in his and looked up at me smilingly. "Hello there, Bree." He pushed the hair out of my eyes, lightly tapping me on the nose to make me smile. "Not panicking too much, I hope."

"I don't know..." I admitted. "The Dark Sorceress sounds like a pretty powerful person..."

"Not to worry." Logan squeezed my hand. "We'll get her. We'll fix you. We'll get through this – just as we always do." He sighed heavily. "Oh, Bree – I was so worried about you when Clariss stabbed you. I kept torturing myself, thinking *what if I had prevented it?* What if I had seen it coming – to throw myself in the dagger's path. Instead I tried to save her, to talk her down. I should have known she was evil – I should have known to watch our back. Instead I saw Clariss, just this girl we grew up with back in high school, not some horrible Dark Sorceress...I just didn't really put two and two together..."

"Clariss..." I thought back to the

mountainside; I could feel the wound in my stomach burning with the memory of its pain. "What happened to her? After she stabbed me, I mean..."

"She just...vanished," Logan mused. "Disappeared into smoke. We couldn't even go after her – although we did try to look, we could find no trace of her. So we thought we had to find someplace for you to recover. Rose was able to heal you temporarily, but you still seemed sick. You started turning pale; your body would get ice-cold. Alistair suggested we make a stop in Autumn Springs to cure you. Better than letting word get out in Feyland that their Queen was ill. Plus, this is an incredible powerful place for magic – some of the best alchemists and medicine fairies in all of Feyland come from here. And if anyone can help you or heal you, it would be the people of Autumn Springs..."

"So!" A rumbling, kind voice echoed through the room. "Is the Queen up – is that so?" I turned to see the source of this great booming voice: it belonged to an affably handsome middle-aged man with pale blonde hair and shining eyes. A moment's glance told me enough – this man had to be Alistair's uncle. The two looked almost identical: only age separated the older Duke's features from his young nephew's.

"Breena!" Another voice sounded through the door – this time a familiar one that made my heart leap with joy. Kian rushed through the threshold, sheer love and longing on his face. He ran to me, enveloping me in his arms, kissing me passionately. I stiffened automatically. I couldn't hold back a shiver. Suddenly, Kian felt icy cold to the touch – his skin froze and burned at the same time. I recoiled instinctively, violently, pushing him away.

"What was that?" Kian looked at me, concerned. "What just happened? Are you okay, Breena?" He sighed. "Was this about our fight? Please, Breena – I'm so sorry....I was jealous, I was angry, I didn't mean any of it..."

I shook my head. "No, it wasn't anything like that. I forgive you for that – and I'm sorry, too. It was automatic. Like something in my body. You felt so...cold. Freezing."

Kian furrowed his brow, a look of concern coming over his face. "You were poisoned by the

RALEIGH COUNTY PUBLIC LIBRARY

Dark Sorceress," he said. "But we did not have any knowledge of what kind of poison it was – or its effects. Was your blood green?"

I nodded mutely.

"And now we have another side effect," said the Duke gravely. "Now it appears she feels the chill of winter the way a mortal does. As a Fey, she was immune to the cold of Kian's touch. But now she responds as a mortal would."

"What?" Kian leaped to his feet in shock and surprise. "You're trying to tell me that Breena will freeze up every time she comes near me?"

"And what about the Winter Kingdom?" I couldn't resist breaking in. "We planned to live there – how am I supposed to go back to the Winter Kingdom if I can't deal with the cold. Not to mention...we're supposed to be getting married."

"Breena is now the Queen of All Feyland," Kian insisted, "she cannot have an aversion to Winter – it's part of her kingdom, too."

"Now, now," the Duke said. "Please, do not panic. It may seem like these side effects are severe, but we have the best alchemists in the land working

RALEIGH COUNTY PUBLIC LIBRARY

on Breena; we are working to cure her and to reverse the effects as swiftly as possible. But if she was poisoned by the Dark Sorceress as you said..."

"Uncle!" Alistair's bright, clear voice called out through the doorway. "If I may – if you don't mind – I would like to take a look at Breena myself. She's been asleep for a few days and so we haven't really been able to see the effects of the poison until now. I, too, have been feeling affected – but I was able to read some of the Book before it poisoned me. Maybe the book has the clues we need for understanding the Sorceress's magic."

Alistair had the book under his arm. He walked towards me, putting out a hand to feel my forehead. But no sooner had he come near me than I began to feel a sudden, horrible chill, a sickening feeling at the pit of my stomach.

The second Alistair touched me, I felt a rush of dark energy coursing through me – a transference of power between Alistair and myself. Darkness seemed to fill my veins to bursting; darkness was all around me. Alistair had been able to withstand the magic of the Book somewhat – his alchemical training had strengthened him – but somehow the Book's proximity to me was enough to send me reeling. I felt as if I had been hit by a tidal wave of magic. I started shaking.

"Breena? Breena, what's wrong!" Kian called. But I was writhing, convulsing violently.

The last thing I saw was a puff of black smoke surrounding me, and the astonished faces of Logan, Kian, Alistair and the Duke.

And then they were gone. Or, more accurately, I was gone. I was in an unfamiliar room, staring at an all too familiar face.

"Hello again, Breena, my dear."

Clariss was sitting calmly before me, my crown glinting on her head. "We're going to have a lot of fun together, you and I."

Chapter 5

❄

I was reeling. Smoke was all around me, clogging up my nostrils, filling my field of vision. I staggered backwards, coughing. I put a hand to my mouth as I looked up, waving away the smoke with my other hand. Where was this place? I was in a dark stone room, the only source of light a glimmering candle that shone with a green flame. I felt my stomach drop. My blood was burning; I felt dizzy – nauseous – ill. What was going on?

"Breena, Breena, Breena," Clariss turned to me with a wicked smile. "It looks like you have recovered from my...what's the word? Welcome embrace?"

I jumped in surprise. How had Clariss gotten hold of me? What was I doing here? I swallowed hard, trying to keep my fear off my face. "If you call stabbing me with a poisonous dagger your brand of a welcome embrace, then spare me from getting to know you better." Clariss smiled grimly. "Clariss, what's going on? Why did you bring me here?"

"What can I say?" Clariss laughed. "I'm a show-off, Breena! I wanted to show you just how easy it is to control you when I want to. See? I took you out of your supposedly safe circle of friends back there in Autumn Springs, plucked you out and put you here in front of me. At my mercy. I could stab you, you know. If I wanted. Or worse. I'm trying to think of something worse – but you see, Breena? I don't have to."

Her eyes travelled down to my wrist; I followed her gaze. I gasped in shock. My skin had gone pale, pallid white, and through the skin I could see that my veins had turned indigo. A chill travelled through me. "I can see how my poison is affecting you, Breena," Clariss smiled. "You're freezing, aren't you?"

"Freezing?"

"Blue blood. A mysterious chill. And you haven't figured it out? Silly girl. You and your supposedly clever magical friends – the Duke of Autumn Springs. King Kian himself. And none of them can figure it out."

I said nothing, although my heart was pounding. I wanted to hear more, but I wouldn't give Clariss the satisfaction of knowing that I was interested in what she had to say.

"But I know more than any of you. My magic stems from the very beginning of Feyland itself, stretching back to its very core. I am possessed of the kind of ancient Fey magic that was strong enough to create the seasons for all the world. Summer, Winter, Spring, Summer. Not just in this world, but in the mortal world. *Your* world," she spat. "You do know that the Fey control both seasons – including the seasons of your precious Gregory, don't you?"

I had heard legends that the Fey had power in the Land Beyond the Crystal River. I nodded slowly. "What does this have to do with the poison you have in me?" I sighed. "And in Alistair?"

"What matters," said Clariss lightly, "Is that there is no amount of magic that your Fey friends can have capable of curing the poison. The only way to cure you is if I *choose* to remove it."

"I'm listening." I glared at Clariss. She licked her lips and sat down by my side.

"Now, why should I remove it, you may ask?"

"I didn't," I muttered.

"Now, now; don't sulk," Clariss laughed. "I'll tell you. I'm not going to kill you, Breena. Not now, at any rate. I like making you weak. I like watching you squirm, watching your fear. I like making it impossible for you to lie alongside your love, to be in his arms, without your blood freezing within your veins. Soon you'll have to be far away from him – even his touch will cause you to cry out in agony."

I gulped. So it was true. Clariss' spell would make it impossible for me to touch Kian. I looked up at Clariss and choked back the rage within me. I wanted to hit her, to strangle her, to choke her life out. But I had to stay calm – to bear through this chaos – in order to get answers. What was this poison? And why was Clariss here?

I decided to play along, although it took every ounce of my self-control to do it. "That sure was clever, Clariss. I should have known. You were always so smart. Perhaps that was why I was so jealous of you all along." I swallowed, trying to arrange my features so that this appalling lie took on something of the character of truth. "You've always been so smart, so pretty..."

Clariss' expression softened, briefly. Her smile became almost genuine.

"What do you want me to do, Clariss? Why do you want me? Why am I here?"

"What a fool you are!" Clariss rolled her eyes. "You're Queen of Feyland and you don't even understand. You don't know what it's like to be Fey. You don't even know the ancient Fey lore – everything the Queens knew for centuries: Feyland is ruled by the seasons, Winter Fey, Summer Fey, Autumn, and Spring. The seasons are controlled in Feyland and Gregory by what? You should know this.

I tried to think. "The Fey," I said.

Clariss roared with laughter before sneering, "You're a disgrace to your kind, a miserable half-breed..."

"You're one to talk!" I couldn't resist snapping back. "You're not even Fey at all, are you?"

Spring Frost: Frost #7

"I'm not! I'm..." Clariss stopped, her lips curling into a dark smile. "I'm something higher than that, a kind you could never even dream of. But I won't tell you. I won't give away the secret. Not yet. You'll have to figure it out for yourself. I gave you one of the biggest clues already, but you're too stupid to figure it out."

I cursed inwardly. "If you're not even Fey," I asked, "then why come here? Why try to rule over us? What can you possibly get out of it? Why not just...find power in our world?"

"Because, Breena," Clariss looked frustrated, as if she were explaining this to a kindergartner. Good, I thought. Let her think I'm dumb. Maybe then she'll talk. "Although I am not Fey, as you say, I am from here. But I don't see why I should waste my breath explaining all this to you. Let it suffice to say that this is why you're here with me right now. To present a challenge to you and your friends. I heard you thought you were a pixie, stupid girl! Pixies' blood is green – but yours is blue. You think you're clever – defeating my Dark Hordes, bringing back the Twin Suns of Feyland when I had my Hordes squeeze them out like shrivelled oranges – but you will not dare to defy me this time. I want Feyland. And in order to get that desire, my dear friend Breena, I want you. So let me tell you my plan, which you – if you want to live – will help me with. I will rule on the throne of Feyland, with Logan the Wolf Prince as my Consort. The people of Feyland – although who knows why? – love you. They respect you. They listen to whatever you have to say. So, Breena, when I arrive as a guest in your kingdom, you will welcome me with all the warmth and hospitality your foolish little heart can muster. You will make the people love me. And then *I* will be Queen of Feyland."

I looked at Clariss in shock. My mouth dropped open. Could she be serious? Could Clariss really think that I would be willing to help her take over my kingdom? "I would rather die!" I spat.

"I can grant you that wish, Breena," sighed Clariss. "But there's no need. You're dying already. The blue-green tint in your blood proves that: it shows the poison coursing through your veins. Once it turns black, you see, you will be nothing more than a shadow figure, one of those Dark Hordes, under my command. And then I'll control you anyway." She smiled sweetly. "You see, Breena, you have no choices. Heads, I win. Tails, you lose. But you have a way out here, don't you see that? You could help me. If you help me get the people of Feyland to accept me as their Queen, we can avoid so much *unnecessary* bloodshed, don't you think? I can help to restore your land, to make it beautiful again, to restore all the darkness that has destroyed it. I can also save your friend Alistair, keep his mind from being devoured by the poison he has consumed. He is a strong one – that's why he was able to read the book in the first place – but he is no match for my dark magic. He will go mad, Breena; mark my words. He will go mad if he does not a get a cure from me, and once he goes mad he will become so wild, so dangerous that you will have no choice but to slay him. To murder your own friend in cold blood. And how would pretty little Rose feel about that? It would break her innocent little heart. So I am giving you a choice, Breena. Because I am kind. Because I am merciful. Either you pave the way for me to smoothly take over Feyland, allowing me to save

Alistair's life and – if you're *very* good – your own. You can go back to your mommy. You can go quietly. Or else you can die, and become one of the mindless Dark Hordes that do my bidding." She chuckled. "Guess you didn't expect that out of me, did you, Breena? But I tell you – being me has its privileges!"

I sat quietly, taking Clariss' words in. I knew in my heart that I had only one option. No matter the costs, I would have to stay strong. Better to die loyal to Feyland than to live having betrayed it. This was my country – my land. These were my people. They depended on me. I looked up at Clariss, my crown glittering and glimmering on her head. I sighed. No, Clariss could never be allowed to rule Feyland. All that talk about restoring the land's beauty was, I knew, a lie. She could never be trusted. But I'd have to play along. I'd have to outsmart her. Before the poison took over me.

"You've always wanted what I have," I said softly. "Logan, my power, my title. But I didn't need it. I don't need it – not any of it. Logan loved me before I ever came close to a crown. My friends respected me no matter what. I don't mind giving up

Feyland to you. I don't need Feyland to make me happy. And, of course, you do deserve it more. You were always more powerful than I was. More beautiful."

I could see Clariss' thin veneer crack. "Really?"

"Of course," I said. "I always thought this crown should go to someone like you – you deserve it much more than me. If you get me back to my friends, I can start preparing your entrance. I'm not stupid, Clariss. I know when I'm beaten. Just let me live – me and my friends – and Kian and I will find someplace quiet to live in Gregory and never bother you again." The words were like ashes in my tongue. I didn't mean them, but the very act of pretending to acquiesce to Clariss' request made me ill. I wanted to tear her hair out. Yet another part of me pitied her – pitied the look of genuine joy in her eyes when I told her that she was prettier than I was. Could Clariss really be driven by such base motives as jealousy?

"Come on, Clariss?" I nodded. "My Queen. Won't you let me go home?"

She turned to me.

She nodded.

Chapter 6

Another puff of smoke surrounded me, this time coming straight from Clariss' finger-tips. I closed my eyes, coughing and wheezing as the world seemed to whirl around me. I looked around in surprise, stretching out my hands until I felt the soft, cool white bed sheets beneath me. I was back in my room in Autumn Springs.

"Clariss?" I looked around me wildly, terrified that she might have followed me here. But, to my relief, Clariss was nowhere to be found. Instead, I was staring at a sea of worried faces. Kian, Logan, the Duke, Alistair, and Rose were all standing around my bedside. I saw that Kian and Logan were conversing quietly, evidently worried. Both had looks of pain and concern upon their faces. But when they saw me, they both looked up, their faces breaking out into a smile.

"Breena!" Kian rushed to my side. "We were so worried. You disappeared just the way Clariss did – into a puff of smoke."

"We didn't even know where to start looking for you," Logan broke in. "We were consulting the books, trying to figure out how the magic worked – but luckily you're back."

"How long was I gone?" I asked.

"About an hour," Rose looked at the clock. She had her arm around Alistair, who was huddled in a corner, looking somewhat overwhelmed by the situation. My heart sank for him. The poison was getting worse for him – I could see it in his eyes. Soon the madness would start up again.

"My friends..." I began. As I looked at them, my heart seemed to swell with pride. Kian and Logan were no longer enemies, I saw, but rather working together. Rose was tending to Alistair. No, I thought – I could never let them down, not in a million years. Not if it meant my own life. But nor could I let Clariss rule Feyland. There had to be another way. I could never concede to Clariss – I couldn't let her win...

Spring Frost: Frost #7

"Come," the Duke of Autumn Springs approached me, bowing at my bedside. "You must be starving, Breena. Between your illness and your recent...incident...you haven't eaten in days."

No sooner had he spoken than I realized just how hungry I was. My stomach rumbled loudly in response; my whole body felt weak. Lightheaded.

"The morning meal is ready, and I am sure that you are starving, my Queen."

"Starving," I said, forcing out a smile.

The Duke took my hand and led us down the corridor, into an intricately carved hallway lined with the most exquisite tapestries I had ever seen. We followed the woven carpet down the hall and into a room filled with mirrors, in which a single table – piled high with all manner of pastries and savory dishes – was reflected hundreds of times, so that it looked like a whole sea of tables awaited our banqueting. The smell of the food – overpowering in its aroma – made me dizzy and ravenous at the same time.

"Careful," Logan pushed me upright. "You need to take it slow, Bree."

Shasta and Rodney were already seated at the table, and from the looks of it had already gone through two bowls of soup each.

"Come now, my love." Kian put his arm around me. Instantly I jumped, feeling the shiver of ice down my back. I stopped to catch my breath.

"Kian, I'm sorry…" I sighed. "I don't know what's come over me." I leaned in to kiss him, but his lips seemed to freeze my own. How could I tell him what I had learned from Clariss? How could I tell him what was wrong with me?

"Is it…me?"

"We'll talk about it later," I said. I could not meet his eyes. Kind, gentle Kian loved me so much – how could I admit to him that his very caresses were the source of my pain? I couldn't bear to think about the look in his eyes when I told him that he couldn't touch me, that I could no longer feel his smooth skin against my own, that I could no longer listen to the sound of his heartbeat…

"Good food, huh?" Rose was trying hard to minimize the awkwardness, digging into her plate of eggs with gusto. "I mean, delicious!" Her voice shattered the silence. I knew how hard she was trying – trying to make us all forget about the shadow that the Sorceress had cast over us, but no amount of eggs or soup or bread was going to make me forget the truth: the poison was coursing through my veins. Every second I spent not chasing Clariss down was one second off my life.

Where did you go?

I looked up in surprise. And then I realized the voice had not come from without but from within: Kian's voice was echoing in my brain. He hadn't communicated like that with me in days.

What?

Just now. I know you don't want to worry the others, Breena – but you have to know...you can always be honest with me. Trust me with your secret. Please tell me what happened.

I don't know where I was...when Alistair came at me with the book, something happened. I felt this jerk on the back of my neck, and then I was gone. Wherever I was, Clariss was there.

She's alive? I could see Kian's expression turn to fear. *Breena, are you okay? Did she do anything to you?*

I shook my head. *She didn't have to,* I said.

What do you mean?

*The poison...*I bit my lip. *There's no cure, is there, Kian? Her magic's strong, ancient, and powerful. It's causing me to Freeze.* I sighed. I didn't want to hurt him – but lying to him would be worse. *It's why I'm responding the way I am when you touch me. The poison...she said it would make me into one of the Dark Hordes.*

No! It cannot be. Kian was trying desperately hard to keep his expression neutral so that none of the others would be able to tell that we were speaking, but I saw how he strained with the effort. *Breena – tell me it is not so! I have heard of Freezing in some of the old magic books, but I always thought it was just a legend...too horrible to be real...*

So Freezing did exist, then, I thought grimly. Clariss hadn't just been making it up out of nowhere.

She's offered to spare my life, Kian. All of ours – and Alistair's. But on one condition. A terrible condition. She wants me to give up my throne, to make her the Ruler of Feyland.

Kian rose to his feet, smashing his goblet against the wall with rage. The others looked at him in surprise and shock.

"Kian?" Shasta turned to him. "Are you okay? What happened..."

We can't tell them.

Kian caught my eye and nodded furtively. "I'm fine, Shasta. I'm just stressed, that's all. I let my emotions get the better of me for the moment – that is all. Don't worry about it."

"Right..."

We continued eating the meal in silence.

What did you tell her?

I lied – of course! I told her I'd help her – thought I'd try to learn all I could, gather information. But if I have to, Kian, I'd rather die than think of that...witch controlling Feyland.

*Breena, I will love you whatever you decide. But I can't bear to think of losing you. I would rather love you with no title than lose you...*he sighed. *But I* *know you cannot lose your honor. And neither can I. We must stay strong, for Feyland.*

Yes. For Feyland.

I will do what I can. This cannot be the only option. We have strong magic between us. We will find a way to fight this poison within you, Breena. With or without Clariss. And we will destroy this threat to Feyland, Breena. Just as we always do – fear not. I have confidence that we'll get through this.

But I could see the fear on his face – and he the fear in mine. We both had our doubts: we had fought evil before, but the Sorceress was a greater danger than any we could have ever imagined. And if even Rose and Alistair – two of the most skilled alchemists in all of Feyland – couldn't figure out what was wrong with me, or how to fix it, then how could I ever expect to live?

"Now!" Kian announced. "Breena has recovered from her injuries now – and so we must head off to the Winter Kingdom as soon as possible. Feyland must not be without a leader. And if we set off now, I have no doubt that we will be able to make good time and arrive in the Winter Court by tonight.

So I must ask you all to begin packing. Sire," he turned to the Duke, "thank you again for your hospitality, your kindness and discretion. May Autumn Springs always be a great friend of ours. You are always welcome in both Winter and Summer, and you must only say the word and we shall repay your kindness many fold."

The Duke bowed deeply. "It is an honor to serve the King and Queen of Feyland," he said.

We all retreated back to our rooms, quickly packing up our things for the journey. But as I returned to my room, I noticed a shadowy figure following me – only a few paces behind me. Clariss?

I turned around in surprise. "Alistair? What are you doing here?"

Alistair looked nervous, his eyes downcast. He could not meet my gaze. The book was in his arms, wrapped tightly to his chest. "Nothing, Breena..." he said, stumbling over the words. "I just left my coat in your room, that's all."

But there was something about Alistair's gaze and voice that frightened me. I remembered what

Clariss had said about Alistair going mad, and I shivered.

Chapter 7

I dressed hurriedly. My customary silks and satins were not enough to shut out the freeze I felt deep within my body. I huddled under the blankets, scrounging through my wardrobe for the warmest-looking furs I could find. But nothing could make me stop shivering. *Is this it?* I wondered. *Is this going to be my life from now on* – or, at least, what was left of it? I shuddered and looked down. My veins were pulsing: great blue lines snaking out through my skin, which had become almost translucent with sickness. I wanted to be sick. I wasn't beautiful any longer, I thought, nor strong: this Freeze was turning me, little by little, into a grotesque creature. Soon, I knew, my blood would turn black and turgid; soon it would all be over. I closed my eyes as I passed by the mirror. I didn't want to see the sick, hollow, gaunt look in my eyes. I didn't want to see this dying version of myself.

Kailin Gow

There was a solution – of course. I could bow down to Clariss, hand over to her the kingdom and the title and the power and the rest of it. She would – or at least, she *said* she would – let me go free. Kian and I could live alone in Gregory: simple, free. Happy. But I sighed at the very thought, shaking my head. Of course Kian and I could never be happy living out the rest of our lives in ignominy and despair, knowing that just beyond the Crystal River, Feyland was suffering beneath the tyranny of Clariss.

You and I are alike, Kian I thought glumly. *Neither one of us can live without honor. We would rather give everything else up – but not that.* I looked out the window, casting my glance over Autumn Springs towards Feyland in the distance. The suns had returned; two gleaming balls of brightness spread out over the horizon. *So beautiful,* I thought to myself. *Too beautiful.* How could I let myself think, even for a moment, that I would allow Clariss to cast a shadow over the lands – over the hills and valleys, the sweet springs and the violent waterfalls – that I so loved? No, I thought, gritting my teeth. Better to die in a Feyland that was still beautiful than to live outside it, my heart torn out by grief and despair.

But even if I died...would it really save Feyland? My jaw clenched; my heart began to beat faster. If I died, what was to stop Clariss from sauntering in and taking over Feyland, sitting upon *my* throne, wearing *my* crown. What would happen to my king, my Kian? My body began to tense with rage at the very thought! I trusted Kian and Logan – I trusted my armies. But what if they weren't enough? What if the Dark Hordes returned – this time, as Clariss had said, with I myself at the helm? Would I spend the rest of eternity a shapeless zombie, performing Clariss' wicked will? Such a thought was too dire for me to think about. The Dark Sorceress' powers were the greatest we had faced in all our struggles before. She was the conjurer of the Dark Hordes. Her magic transcended life and death, immortality and mortality, and the borders between worlds. Combined that with the vengeful evil wrath of Clariss, the one human without a sense of humanity, she was too powerful to defeat. She made the Dark

Hordes, took away the Twin Suns, and caused all of Feyland to die. How was I going to defeat her?

Tears came to my eyes – savage blue tears, tinted by the poison in my blood. Was this to be the end of Feyland? There had to be another way – there was *always* another way! Had Kian and I – not to mention Logan, Alistair, Shasta, Rodney, and Rose – not suffered enough, overcome enough obstacles to be together and to save Feyland? Would there always be some new danger, some new threat on the horizon? Even if we did manage to cure me, to hold of Clariss, would some new danger, lurking in the shadows, appear to destroy us all? We were fighting a losing game with evil: a game we would never win.

Is this how it ends? Evil triumphing over good? The wicked finishing last?

I wiped the tears from my eyes, as hurriedly as I could. I didn't want anyone else to see me crying, and with Alistair lurking about, I wasn't safe from prying eyes. Whatever was wrong with Alistair, it wasn't about to get better, not without some serious magic to save him. I sat down on the bed, pushing the hair out of my eyes. I was willing to sacrifice myself – that much was my duty as Queen of Feyland – but could I sacrifice Alistair? Clariss had promised to cure him, after all: could I really be responsible for his madness? Every minute that passed by was another minute for the poison to seep deep within him; every moment that he spent under Clariss' influence was another chance for evil to trickle into his bloodstream. I would spent the remainder of my short life watching, waiting for signs of Alistair's madness, wondering if *this*, *this* were the moment during which I would have to kill him.

A murderous rage rose up within me – inexplicably and yet terrifying. It overwhelmed me; it seemed to take control of my brain, of my body. I was shivering with cold; now I was shaking with anger. A feeling of profound evil, like an electric shock, had passed through me. I looked up at the mirror in shock, gasping as I caught sight of my reflection. I looked cruel. Wicked. Murderous. My light eyes had turned black with hatred. I clasped my hand to my mouth. Was this what I was becoming? Was this what the poison was turning it into?

I rushed from the room, unable to bear the silence a moment longer. I couldn't bear to be left alone with my own thoughts, my own fears.

"Breena!" A voice interrupted me and stopped me straight in my tracks. "Before you go – there's something I want to give you." It was the Duke of Autumn Springs, jovial and kind. There was a look of such warmth in his eyes –it made me ashamed of my fear, of my doubts. I could trust him; I knew. He was worth trusting.

"Yes?" I quickly rearranged my features, hoping that the Duke wouldn't see the nervousness on my face. "What is it?"

Alistair emerged from the shadows. "Can I help you, uncle?"

The Duke sighed. "There is...a potential treatment. Not a cure, mind you. But a potential treatment. Something that could last you a few days, that could slow down the effects of the Freeze. It was prepared many centuries ago by the Enchantress; nobody knows how the potion is made, nor its secret ingredients, though many have tried. I didn't want to get your hopes up, but I have been able to purchase a quantity of this potion through one of the merchants who makes his trade selling in a shop in the village. It should stop the spread of the poison for ten days. Thus, divided between you and Alistair..."

"Five days each," I echoed. "That should be enough to give us a head start on finding a cure."

"No," said Alistair softly. I turned to look at him. His bright blue eyes shone out at me – there was a kindness, a gentleness in his eyes I had not seen for some time. These were the eyes of the true Alistair, not the poisonous creature that had taken over his body. "Ten days," he said. "Ten days for Breena."

"What, Alistair? No, you can't..."

"I know what I'm doing," said Alistair. "It was my own fault for reading that book. My pride led me to believe I was invincible. Feyland needs its Queen, Breena. And I have taken an oath. An oath to serve and protect you. Whatever happens to me..." he swallowed hard, and in that moment he looked younger and more vulnerable than ever before. "I can take it. It's my duty. I won't swallow one drop of that potion, Breena, no matter how hard you try to persuade me. I can promise you that. So you might as well drink it. So there." He crossed his arms, as if to drive the point home.

"Are you...ah...are you sure, Alistair?" The Duke looked worried.

"I am sure." Alistair did not look up.

"In that case...very well..." The Duke turned to me.

"I hope it did not come at too great a price, Your Grace," I said. But the Duke's eyes travelled to a corner of the room, and my gaze followed his. A gorgeous golden statue, which I had recalled only that morning, was now absent from the landing. Sold, no doubt.

"One day I hope to be able to repay you, Your Grace," I said.

"It was nothing," he said. "A trifle. A trinket. The unity and salvation of Feyland – there is no price too great."

"I owe you my life, Duke," I said, trying not to let my voice tremble as I thought about just how short that life would be. "I hope one day I am able to return your kindness. And I am...sorry about Alistair."

The Duke's eyes filled with sadness.

"I'll be fine," said Alistair shortly. "I'll find a cure – for both of us, Breena. And if I don't, well." he laughed darkly. "I've had a good life."

How brave Alistair was – facing his madness without fear! I wished I could assume just a little of his courage.

The Duke handed me a small clear vial filled with orange-red liquid. I eagerly gulped it down. It tasted like honey – a warm, soothing taste that seemed to warm my throat and my insides. A wave of calm swept over me, and I closed my eyes. The murderous rage, the fear, the anger all subsided; I looked down to see my veins – still blue – yet less prominent than before. My skin was returning to a color that imitated health. It wasn't a permanent fix, I knew, but it was better than it had been before.

Ten days.

That was how much time I had. Time to find a cure – or time to prepare for death. I shuddered at the thought. *I have ten days to save Feyland.* It wasn't much time, I knew, but it was all we had.

The sound of the clock chiming reminded me of just how brief that time was.

"It is time for you to set out, Your Highness," said the Duke. "You will want to ensure that you are in the Winter Court by nightfall."

I didn't know what to say. But – in a gesture that broke all rules of royal protocol – I thanked him the only way I knew how. In a great, soulful bear-hug.

"No need for that, Highness," he said. "You'll be fine."

I only wished I could believe him.

Chapter 8

I made my way down to the Great Hall, where the others were already waiting for me. Logan was standing with his arms crossed, looking out of the window with a grave look upon his face. Shasta and Rodney were huddled in a corner; his broad arms enveloped her slender shoulders. They both looked exhausted. I couldn't blame them. Shasta and Rodney had been through so much – our quest to restore the Suns of Feyland had been Shasta's one chance at making amends for the damage she had caused by accidentally summoning the Dark Hordes. But I could see the guilt in her eyes: Shasta was ashamed of her actions, even now. No matter how many heroic actions she performed; no matter how many lives she saved...the look of darkness in Shasta's eyes would never change. She would never forget the cost of that moment of selfishness. It would always haunt her.

Rose brightened when she saw Alistair coming downstairs alongside me, but her expression turned to consternation as Alistair got closer. I couldn't help but feel a twinge of guilt as Rose's eyes settled on Alistair's pallid expression.

"Are you okay, Alistair?" she asked softly. "You look a little..."

"I'll be fine!" Alistair brushed away her concerns with harsh brusqueness. "Don't you worry about me." He did not meet her gaze. There was something sharp, almost cruel in his voice. A touch of Clariss' poison? I couldn't let myself wonder about that.

Poor Alistair, I thought to myself. He had given up his share of the potion – but in so doing he had put a ticking bomb in the midst of his own existence: who knows how much longer he had left to live? But he wasn't about to let on that he was afraid. Instead he stood with his arms crossed and his gaze downcast – Rose, at his side, looked more than a little hurt. Would things never be happy for them, I wondered?

"My love!" Kian bounded over to my side. "How are you feeling, my dearest one? Any better?" He made as if to touch me, but pulled back, his face falling. "Sorry, I almost forgot..."

"No, it's okay," I said. I looked down at my hands – my veins seemed less blue, my skin less white. I tentatively stepped forward, reaching out towards him and taking his hands in mine. I lightly ascended on my tiptoes and kissed him – hesitantly, but sweetly, allowing him to feel the slow burn of my love. It did not hurt as it had done before – or, at least, I could bear the pain – but this time an involuntary shiver made my discomfort clear. "It's better than it was," I said. I felt calmer now. The rage that had characterized my morning had subsided; instead, I felt a rush of inner serenity and strength. I was tired – so tired that my muscles and body ached to sleep – but I knew that time was running out. We had to get to the Winter Court as quickly as possible.

"I don't want to hurt you," said Kian, looking ashamed – as if, somehow, my pain was his fault.

"Being without you hurts me even more," I said. "This pain is better than the pain of not being able to sleep in your arms."

Kian smiled sadly. "But if only we could have both," he said.

"If only, indeed."

We set off a few minutes later, our horses mounted and racing through the leafy forests of Autumn Springs. It was truly a beautiful place, I thought, as my mind struggled to take in its glorious lights and colors: orange, red, yellow leaves all shining like blazing flames around me. Each step the horses took resulted in another delicious crunch of fresh leaves underfoot. The air was perfumed – it smelled like nutmeg and cinnamon and burned oranges. I closed my eyes and enjoyed the breeze, all the while trying to avoid the suggestion – gnawing at the back of my mind – that this might be the last time I ever felt it whipping upon my face.

Then it grew colder. As we left the perimeters of Autumn Springs and headed into Feyland proper, we began to catch sight of the snow banks – silvery and white – in the distance. I began to shake – at first it was only a small tremble, my hands fumbling with the horse's reins. Snowflakes were gliding down onto my shoulders; the air was crisp with the scent of pine and fir. I tried to ignore the cold, tried to ignore the way my hands were turning blue, but it was to no avail. Soon I was shivering – several swift, sharp shivers that seemed to turn my spine into jelly.

"Breena, what's going on?" Kian looked up, worried.

"It's fine," I responded. "Just keep riding, please. We need to get there faster..."

"Not if it's harming your health!" Kian said. He immediately removed his fur coat, letting it fall to the snow. "You need to wear this," he said, handing it to me and wrapping it around my shoulders. His touch made me shake even more violently. "I'm trying not to touch you," he said, his voice trembling as much as my body. "I just want to comfort you so badly, to make this better..."

Logan averted his eyes. I did not want to see the pain in his gaze, and so I looked away, too.

"I can't do this..." Kian sighed. "I can't not touch you."

I wrapped the fur tighter around my shoulders. "The fur is warming me up," I said. "I'm just getting used to the Winter Kingdom. It'll be better soon; I'm sure of it."

"How can I be sure?" Kian's eyes were like saucers.

"We need to build a fire," Rose said. "Take an hour's rest. We've got four hours of riding until we get to the Kingdom – we'll be there tonight, at least. But it's more important that we don't risk Breena's health."

"No – we have to hurry..." I protested. The last thing I wanted was to slow down the others, especially when I was sure that nothing the others did would work: Clariss' poison was a one-way ticket to the Dark Hordes, and no amount of fur or fire could fix that.

"Nonsense," said Rose. "Executive decision, we're taking a rest." She dismounted her steed. "Shasta and Rodney – you start building a fire. Kian, let's go hunting for some dinner. Logan, you help

Breena off her horse – Breena, don't protest, there's no way you can dismount in this state."

Logan nodded curtly and dismounted his own horse, coming over to my side. He put his hands around my waist. "Ready, Breena?" he turned to me with a small smile.

I started. Something – a strange, warm sensation – had stirred within me. It felt like I had taken the potion again – only stronger. A feeling of red, powerful warmth stirring through me. His hands were like hot stones, warming my flesh. Immediately I stopped shaking, my body responding to his as he placed me gingerly down upon the ground.

"What is it?" Kian turned to me. "Did something happen? Is he hurting you?"

"No..." I looked up at Logan in confusion. "Not at all. The...opposite, actually."

"What do you mean?" Kian came over to us, looking Logan up and down.

"It stops the cold," I admitted sheepishly, not wanting Kian to see how red my face had gotten. He'd been jealous enough of Logan in the past – the last thing I wanted was to make things worse. "Something about Logan...it makes me warmer."

Kian looked perplexed. "How could that be?"

"Perhaps it's because he's not a Fey," Rose chimed in. "Or at least, not-really. He's the closest to mortal – indeed, his blood is even warmer because of his Wolf side. Maybe he can warm Breena up while the rest of us are making her worse."

Kian considered. I could see the wheels of his mind turning – I could see him balance his jealousy of Logan with his need to keep me safe. I knew that even watching Logan's arms around me was torture for him. But the sensation of Logan's touch – hot, spirited, alive – was the only thing keeping the Freeze from getting worse.

"In that case," he said, "you should ride with the Queen, Logan. Keep her warm as best you can. Stay by her side. Do you need a fire, my darling? Or is Logan...preferable?"

"I don't think a fire would work," I admitted. "At least, not as well as what Logan's doing now. It's a magic-thing...his magic's interacting with mine."

Spring Frost: Frost #7

"Very well," Kian said curtly, jumping upon his horse's back anew. "Then let's ride on. There's no use wasting time." I could see how hurt he was, but I knew that there was nothing I could say.

Logan and I mounted the same horse – my own – while Logan's steed, ever-obedient, trotted behind.

"Thanks for this, Logan…" I said, blushing slightly as he wrapped his arm around my waist.

"Anytime, Breena," Logan said, brushing a strand of hair out of my eyes. "I know this isn't easy for you. But whatever I can do to help, to keep you safe…I'll do it. After all, I guess I owe you one."

We fell silent. With everything that had happened, we hadn't talked much about the events on the mountain. Logan had been injured – I had offered to sacrifice my life, my immortality, for his recovery. A decision that I could tell, even now, struck Kian to the bone: Kian's face told me that much. A decision that had led Kian, in a moment of anger, to cancel our wedding.

Kian hadn't meant it, I knew – but if Clariss hadn't come, who knew what would have happened?

My life, my marriage – all placed on hold because I couldn't let Logan go.

"Don't mention it," I said. "It's what friends do for each other. We have a pact, you and I. We make sure that we *both* get out of these situations alive."

"I don't want to get in your way, Breena," said Logan. "If I'd made you unhappy – I'd never forgive myself."

"You could never make me unhappy, Logan," I said. His touch was electric; it was only when in his arms that I realized how much pain I'd been in for the past twenty-four hours. Pain that had, at last, subsided. I felt like myself again. Warm. Safe.

And in Logan's arms.

I caught sight of Kian looking at us, his face frozen in a frown. First I had offered to give my life for Logan, now it was Logan who was the only one able to save my life – while wrapping his arms around me, no less! And all the while Kian was watching me, aching for me, unable to touch me. I wanted to comfort him, to tell him that I loved him no less.

But his touch was dangerous, now.

Spring Frost: Frost #7

I sighed as we rode faster into the Winter Kingdom. Would our struggles ever be at an end?

Chapter 9

The ride back to the Winter Kingdom took longer than we had expected. There were no obstacles in our path, but somehow the stress had taken its toll on all of us, and we could see the first cresting of dawn on the horizon by the time the Winter Court came into view. I sighed as I caught a glimpse of its bright, gleaming spires. The stained glass window – an enormous, flower-shaped structure on the east end of the castle – gleamed with the rising sun, sending patterns of color onto the snow, dancing like rainbows. I gasped at the site. Its beauty cheered me, warmed my heart. My flesh, however, was another story. Logan's touch had stopped the Freezing, at least temporarily, but I knew in my heart that it was no permanent solution.

Spring Frost: Frost #7

"It's beautiful, isn't it?" Shasta breathed softly, looking all around her. "I mean, last time I was here..." Her voice trailed off and her expression tinged with sadness. "Last time I was here it was dark. There was so much destruction, so much death...now at least they have hope. *We* have hope." She looked up at Rodney, who squeezed her hand and smiled at her, love in his eyes. "When we left here we didn't know if the suns would ever shine again on Feyland – and now, look!" She made a motion towards the sky. "Two of them, shining more brightly than ever before." She turned to me. "We're all scared of this Sorceress, Breena. Me as much as anyone else. But at the same time...we can't forget all the good we've done. The war between Winter and Summer is over. The suns are restored. Whatever happens, we'll at least have succeeded in that."

"Sometimes it seems like the evil's too great," admitted Logan. "Like no matter how much we do, no matter how hard we fight – there's always more to do. I don't know if we'll ever get to just...you know...rest."

Kian and I exchanged glances. We knew as much as anyone did how strong the desire for rest was. Only a few weeks ago I'd dreamed of marrying Kian, of making a life with him. I had agreed to be his bride. But now it seemed that our dream would be put on hold for the foreseeable future. I turned to Shasta and sighed. Surely the same was true for her and Rodney – more true, in fact, since she and Rodney had been together even longer. We were all waiting for the troubles to end – to go home to the people we loved. Me to Kian. Rodney to Shasta. Alistair to Rose. Logan drew in breath sharply and I turned back to him.

Poor Logan, I thought. Even when all this was over, even when we defeated this Sorceress (*if* we defeated this sorceress – but I couldn't dwell on that!), then he'd have nobody to go back to. Part of me wished that I could find someone out there for him, someone for Logan to love who could love him as fully and undividedly as I could not. But Logan's loyalty made it impossible; I would have his heart no matter what. Even if I didn't want it.

Spring Frost: Frost #7

Or did I want it? I couldn't deny that the feeling of his arms around me made me tingle, ever so slightly. It was a comfortable, familiar feeling. But having him so close to me only made me more aware of what I could not give him, of what I could never give him. If I loved him at all, I knew – I would have to let him go. Let him find love somewhere else.

Was it hard for him, I wondered? Being among all these couples. Granted, Rose and Alistair hadn't exactly verbalized their attraction – although I was pretty sure that what I saw in Alistair's eyes was nothing short of puppy love – but they definitely had some serious tension between them. And Logan remained so noble, so solemn and strong, even as I knew his heart was breaking inside. My heart ached for him, for his pain. *If only there was some way I could make it all go away.* But I knew deep down that the only way to make it okay in his heart was to succumb to his love: a choice I could never make.

We made our way into the palace. There, we were greeted by Silverwing, a young attendant whom I recognized from our visit with the Winter Queen some months ago.

"Greetings, your Highness," said Silverwing, bowing to me and to Kian.

"How has the palace been getting on in our absence?" asked Kian brusquely. "Are the lands recovering?"

Silverwing smiled broadly. "Yes, your Highness. The day the suns returned to the sky there was a great day of feasting – for we knew that our King and Queen had saved us!"

"Not just us," I cut in. "Rose and Rodney and Shasta and Alistair and...Logan. They were all part of the effort."

"The crops began to grow anew," Silverwing looked overjoyed. "And for three days and nights we celebrated. Winter and Summer together took to the fields to begin sowing new seeds and reaping fruit and vegetables that grew overnight – the magic of the earth restored."

"Together?" Kian smiled wryly. "See what we have wrought, my darling? Who would have imagined it? A few years ago they would have called us mad to predict that Summer and Winter would harvest the same fields, reap the same crops. But now look! Can you not see it?" He kissed me and I did my best not to recoil. My body ached for him even as I feared his touch; the more I thought of the pain that would shudder through me, the more I desired it, for at least that pain meant that my love was near me. I knew too that Kian was trying to cheer me up – if these were to be my last days alive, I thought bitterly – then at least I'd want to know that I'd done something useful in my life.

Perhaps I had. As I looked around at the courtiers, I couldn't help but smile. One by one they brought sumptuous dishes forth – a breakfast even more lavish and luxurious than the one we had eaten the previous day in Autumn Springs. There was something vaguely comforting about being in the Winter Court, among friends at last. The good food warmed my spirit, if not my body. But more important still was the sight of my old friends and subjects – together at last. At least one third of the attendants at the Winter Court were people I recognized from the Summer Court, and seeing them working together, seeing Summer and Winter as friends at last, made me feel as if my life were worth something, after all. *Even if I do die,* I told myself, *at least I've accomplished something. At least I've accomplished this.* I didn't want to die – I didn't feel ready. But as I looked around me I knew that, whether or not I survived this, Feyland would. Whatever Clariss brought against us, whatever tactics she used – we would beat her together. Clariss may be strong, but the combined power of Feyland would be stronger. She would never overpower this great land.

I looked over at Kian and his eyes were blazing with love. In his gaze I could see all of his pride, all of his happiness, at seeing his homeland reunited once more. "Come, my lady," he whispered in my ear. "You're looking distractingly lovely. Might I steal you away?"

We looked around, but the others were too busy eating and drinking to notice us. We slipped away to Kian's bedroom, a room I recognized from my previous visit. The sheets were silver and blue; the walls were lined with exquisite silver carvings, the floor with marble.

"Shall I light a fire to warm you?" He had only to say the word, and then the fireplace blazed with hot, sultry light. "We don't have to touch if it hurts you, Breena. We can just sit together, in front of the fire."

"No suffering can be as great as *not* touching you, Kian," I explained. "Logan may be able to warm my body – but he doesn't have my heart. You do, Kian. You know that."

Kian smiled sadly. "I believe you," he said. "But sometimes I wonder..."

"Are you still jealous? Because of what happened at the mountain?"

Kian sighed. "Not jealous," he said at last. "Only..."

"Only what?"

"I don't ever want you to feel that you *have* to be with me. If I don't make you happy..."

"Believe me," I said, "if I feel that I have to be with you, it's only because my body and soul alike are telling me that I'd die without you. I *want* to be with you. I care for Logan as a friend – but you..."

Kian nodded.

I leaned in and kissed him, bracing myself for the impact. It was slow and sweet – hesitant at first – but the fire of my passion seemed to drown out the chills. I pulled him towards me, kissing him more roughly, giving into my desire. I could withstand the pain – better the pain than another moment staring into his steel-blue eyes, unable to press my mouth against his...

"Are you sure?" Kian looked surprised.

"I'm sure!"

"It's been too far long!" Kian's telepathic voice echoed into my head, along with his physical voice. It was an intense sensation.

In an instant we were on the bed, tangling our limbs in the silken fabric. His mouth on mine, was the sweetest touch, and then it became hungrier and more passionate. Even with the pain of the cold, I felt more alive, more joyous, than I had since the stabbing. Every fiber of my being ached for Kian and I to become one. If I was going to die, then I had to make the most of the little time I had left. And I wanted to spend that time with him. With the man I loved.

We were interrupted by a frantic knocking on the door.

"Breena, Breena! Kian! Hurry!" Rodney and Shasta's voice distracted us from our passion. Kian leaped to his feet, placing a fur dressing gown around his shoulders.

"What's going on?"

"Hurry!" Shasta cried. "Before he kills him!"

"Kills who? What are you talking about?"

"Alistair! He's got Logan – and he's going to kill him!"

Chapter 10

Kian and I followed Shasta and Rodney, our hearts pounding. Was this the moment we'd been waiting for – the moment during which the madness that had been seeping into Alistair's brain at last overpowered him? I shuddered at the thought. Surely there had to be some hope, something we could do, some power...

But Clariss' words echoed in my brain, haunting me in their cruelty. *One of you will have to slay him.* I thought of Rose – her pale face and her flushed cheeks – would she have to watch as I killed the man she loved? But if there wasn't any cure, I knew, then we had no choice: Alistair would have to die, or else we would all die with him.

Shasta led us back into the dining hall. A throng of people made a circle; we pushed through them hurriedly. There, in the center of the room,

Spring Frost: Frost #7

Alistair was standing upon one of the long tables we had been banqueting on only moments before, pinning Logan to the ground with magic: two long spindles of dark light emerging from his fingertips.

"Alistair?" I tried to keep my voice as gentle as possible so as not to frighten him. "Alistair, what's going on?"

The soothing tone I had attempted to adopt seemed to work. Alistair looked up, distracted – just for a moment. Enough time for Kian to rush at Alistair, attempting to tackle him full-on.

But Alistair looked back down just in time. A single flash of lightning – a black illumination that seemed to blind us all – pushed Kian back against the wall. He fell with a loud crash; my heart briefly stopped. But Kian's moan of pain brought me some relief – he was alive, I thought. At least he was alive.

"Alistair, what are you doing?" I took another step forward, trying not to spook him. "That's Logan – our friend! You know that..."

But another voice interrupted us, coming into the fray. "Alistair!" It was a light, sweet woman's voice. Rose's. "Please, Alistair – just let Logan go, okay?"

Alistair turned to Rose. I saw his face filled with anger, with white-hot rage. I had never seen a face so devoid of humanity: Alistair's smile was a mocking, cruel one, but there was no light in his eyes. There was only anger, only pain. "I know what I saw!" he cried. "I saw you with him, Rose. I know what you were doing."

Kian and I looked at each other in surprise. What was Alistair talking about? But when I followed Rose's gaze, I was even more shocked: Rose was looking straight at *Logan.* Logan? What had Alistair seen?

"I saw the two of you together – so close...you were holding hands, snickering about something, whispering behind my back..."

"What are you talking about, Alistair?" Rose looked genuinely confused. Her eyelids fluttered lightly. "This isn't like you at all. You're not the kind of person to get jealous – or violent. And in any case, Alistair, please believe me – you have nothing to be jealous about!" She took another step towards him, pleading with him: her eyes had grown wide with pity and fear. I couldn't imagine anyone refusing Rose in this state – she looked so soft, so innocent, so pliant. But Alistair wasn't having any of it.

"Nothing?" Alistair laughed – a dark, hollow laugh. "Nothing, really?" His face twitched with anger; his frustration seemed to seethe through the room like dark smoke. "What do you say to that, Logan? Rose says it's "nothing!" Well, is it nothing for you too, eh? Do you feel "nothing"? Is that what you feel?"

Logan and Rose exchanged a quick, almost imperceptible glance. I could see Rose draw in breath sharply, her chest heaving with tension. She was poised, waiting – an inscrutable look upon her face.

"Of course, Alistair!" Logan scrambled up to a sitting position. "You know that. Remember, I was the one who encouraged you to go after Rose. I'm your friend – and you are mine. You know where my heart lies..." Logan shot a sad glance at me, and at my side I could feel Kian stiffen. "Not even magic could change that. Rose knows it too – and she certainly doesn't feel anything either."

Only I noticed Rose colored slightly – very slightly – when she spoke. I too was blushing; I looked down at the floor. I didn't want Kian to see that Logan could still bring the crimson to my cheeks.

"Come on, Alistair!" Rodney stepped forward, placing his broad chest squarely between Alistair and Rose. "You know Rose. You trust her. She's kind-hearted to a fault. She was probably consoling Logan – it's been a stressful time for all of us and you know as well as we do that now is the time for us all to stick together. Rose would never betray your trust like that, would you, Rose?"

Rose stumbled over her words. "N-n-o, of course not! Alistair, let Logan go! You're making something out of nothing."

"Rose is a Harvester Fey," Rodney said. "She knows how to get in touch with the animals – she's the only one of us who can communicate with Logan's Wolf side. That doesn't mean there's anything between them. We all have to do our bit to find a cure, to defeat the Sorceress. We can't get distracted by petty jealousies."

"No," Alistair shook his head, crouching down to the floor. "You don't understand. She's playing with me – they're playing with me?"

"Who's playing with you, Alistair?" Rose stepped forth.

"These images...these faces..." Alistair covered his head with his hand. "I can't stop – I can't stop seeing these faces. Haunting me. Overtaking me. Whenever I close my eyes – I see *her...*" He pointed to Rose, who put her face in her hands. "She's lying to me, betraying me, hurting me..."

"It's not true!" cried Rose. "I never did anything! I promise..."

"It's the poison..." I walked over to Rose, wrapping my arm around her shoulders. "He's hallucinating – seeing visions. That book is driving him mad. It's not the real Alistair..."

Cold comfort, I felt. Kian and his Winter Knights had their swords drawn, ready willing and able to attack at any time. Rose didn't take her eyes off Alistair, staring at him with a soulful gaze. "How do we fix it?" Her voice was small and trembling.

"I don't know," I admitted. "Stand down," I barked to the knights.

Alistair was rocking back and forth on his heels, his head against his knees.

"We've got a clear shot, your Highness," Silverwing said. "He's distracted. We can seize him..."

"No!" cried Rose. "Don't hurt him!"

"Your Highness?" Silverwing asked.

"Wait!" I cried. "We need to see if we can talk him down, first."

Out of the corner of my eye I saw Logan warily scrambling to his feet, taking advantage of Alistair's distraction. He slid backwards, trying to avoid Alistair's gaze.

"Oh no you don't!" Alistair whipped around, his hand shooting out towards Logan's face. Instantly Logan was thrown backwards, hurling through the air until he crashed with a sickening crunch against the stone walls of the palace.

"Logan, no!" I cried. Logan lolled forward, blood pouring from his forehead. Kian rushed to his side, feeling his pulse.

"He's alive!" he called. "But weak. Alistair, you need to…"

"He stands in my way!" roared Alistair. "He took the only thing I've ever loved…"

"What are you…"

"Enough!" An unearthly female voice silenced him, echoing through the room. We all looked in surprise to the source of this great booming voice. It was Rose, speaking in a voice that was not her own. "I said, enough!"

Alistair shot black fire at her, but Rose walked forward, unaffected. She calmly walked towards Alistair and placed her hands around his head. He struggled and shouted, but she was undeterred. She began to sing – chanting in a melodious voice, in a language whose words I did not know. Slowly the light coming from Alistair's eyes and fingers began to dim; a second – white – light appeared around them both. Rodney, Shasta and I looked on in shock and silence. What was Rose – little Rose? – doing?

Alistair began to go slack, his body releasing the tension as he slipped slowly to the ground. His eyes closed and he began to hum softly, rocking back and forth. Rose tightened her grip on Alistair's head, her chanting growing wilder and louder as she held him to her breast like a child.

Alistair slumped over in what looked like a calm sleep. The lights – black and white – vanished.

"What was that?" Rodney looked confused. "Rose, what did you do?"

Rose looked at him with a vacant expression, saying nothing.

"Logan?" I rushed to Logan's side. "Are you okay?" As soon as I touched him I felt his electric warmth seeping through me. "What happened?"

"Is she safe?" Logan was returning to consciousness. "Rose – is she safe?"

"She's right here, she's fine. She saved you."

Logan opened his eyes and looked around. Rose took another step forward. She looked older than before, I noticed – her hair and skin and eyes seemed to be glowing with life and strength and power. This wasn't the same Rose I remembered from my first few visits to the palace. This was a woman of great strength, great magic. Magic that might – I felt, somewhere deep down within me – be greater than my own.

"Rose..." Logan looked up at Rose, his eyes wide. "I wanted to...watch out!"

But he was too late. Alistair had sprung to his feet again and had seized Rose by the neck, a sword – stolen from one of Kian's guards – in his hand. He placed the metal against her throat and she cried out, struggling in vein.

"This isn't Rose!" Alistair spat. "But the Dark Sorceress herself!" He looked around at us. "She's the Sorceress. She's the reason the twin suns disappeared – she's the cause of the destruction and death that followed. She's the evil witch behind all our troubles – she possessed me, made me love her, made me jealous, made me crazy..."

"No!" Rose cried out, struggling harder. "It's not true. I never..."

"She thinks she can possess me, make me crazy – but she's wrong! I know the truth about her now. About her dark powers. She thinks she can just wrap me around her little finger and make me love her. Well, she can't! I'm stronger than all that. I'm stronger than her..."

"Alistair, please!" Rose screamed.

"Let her go, Alistair!" Logan stepped forward.

"Now," Alistair said, his eyes glinting with an evil glow. "In order to remove the poison from me – and from Breena –we have to extinguish and destroy its source. My alchemical training has taught me that much. I'll burn her! We need to destroy the Sorceress completely – make a bonfire of burning rowan oak branches and reduce her to ashes forever."

"Alistair!" Rose tried to scream, but Alistair tightened his grip on her throat and it came out instead in a choked sigh.

"So," Alistair said. "What do you say to starting a bonfire?"

Chapter 11

❄

I looked back and forth between Rose and Alistair in shock. Could what Alistair was saying be true? Rose – the Sorceress? Surely not! She looked so sweet, so innocent – surely she couldn't be another embodiment of Clariss' wicked power. "How do you know she's the Sorceress?" I asked Alistair. "From the likes of it, it sounds like you're the one whose judgement's been clouded recently. You just attacked Logan – why should we believe anything you say?"

Alistair smiled sadly. To my surprise, his entire expression changed. Moments before he had looked animalistic, bestial. But now his sandy golden hair shone bright; his eyes were light and clear. His tanned skin took on a golden glow. He looked handsomer than before, calmer. The look of rage in his eyes subsided. He looked, I thought, like the old

Alistair whom I had previously known. Kian and I traded glances of perplexity: had Alistair been healed? Right now, he looked normal; I could see no sign of evil magic in his eyes.

I blinked, trying to clear my eyes. Was I seeing right? The Alistair that stood before me now – sword in hand notwithstanding – looked far more like the normal Alistair than any incarnation I had seen since he had first read the book.

"I'm sorry for my behavior…" Alistair bowed low. "Queen Breena, I didn't mean to frighten you – or any of you! I'm doing this for your own safety. For our own safety. Just moments ago the poison finally loosed its hold on me, released its grip. But I've been wrong about the source. I've been combing through the Book, thinking that it was the Book that was poisoning me all along. But I was wrong. I've been looking through the Book and I stumbled on a similar potion to the one my uncle gave to you, looking for a way to cure myself. Just a few moments ago I attempted to make the potion with the secret ingredient – and it must have only just started working."

"But you just started fighting Logan!" I stepped forward. "Hardly, it must be considered, the actions of a fully sane man. If you did that after taking the potion..."

"Breena, please!" Rose was calling. She squirmed against his grip, a look of terror on her face. "Breena, please help me!"

"I was angry – overwhelmed – jealous..." Alistair looked at me. "I saw him and Rose – or at least, I thought I saw...these images...these visions...these veils over my brain."

"I told you there was nothing to be jealous about!" shouted Rose. "Now you let me go, or I swear by Autumn Springs I'll give you a reason to be upset!"

"I thought you were my Rose," Alistair sighed. "My sweet Rose – my beloved. But now I know you're an imposter. You're the Dark Sorceress. The potion has liberated me – allowed me to see beyond your glamor. You think you've inflicted your poison in me – it brought me closer to you, at first. It made me hear your thoughts, your wishes. Made me keep an eye on Breena so that you could sense her

- 118 -

whereabouts. But I fought it! I used your book to fight your influence. Now I can use the knowledge I have gleaned to see you as you really are..."

Logan let out an astonished groan. "No wonder..."

"No wonder what?"

Logan turned red. "Nothing – only..."

"What is it?"

"Rose – with me...it wasn't normal. It wasn't like she usually was. Like...Clariss..."

'What are you saying?" Alistair turned to Logan, whipping his head around. "Is it true, then? Did Rose make a move on you?"

Logan hesitated. "No," he said finally. "Not a move – It wasn't a move at all. She was only being kind. Comforting me. I was upset about what happened; she was only being caring, being kind. Asking me if anything was wrong, how I was feeling, innocent stuff like that."

"Innocent stuff?" Alistair looked dubious. "Are you sure?"

"I'm sure." Logan waited for Alistair to look away again.

Spring Frost: Frost #7

"Kind and caring?" I whispered into Logan's ear, quietly enough to ensure that Alistair couldn't hear us. "That doesn't sound too much like Clariss to me."

Logan turned to me with a pained expression on his face. "Listen to me, Breena. Can you meet me outside when all this is over? Out in the gardens? I need to speak to you – alone..."

"Logan?"

"It's important, Bree. Something's up."

I nodded curtly, not wanting the others to see our conversation. "Okay," I said.

"And don't leave Alistair and Rose alone together. Whatever happens – whichever one of them...it's too dangerous, okay?"

I sighed. "Alistair, calm down. If Rose really is the Sorceress, we'll take care of it. Not you. We'll separate you both and figure out what's going on calmly and rationally."

Rose looked horrified. "What?" she cried. "How can you believe him? This crazy, poisoned man..."

"Just let her go," I said, trying to sound firm and decisive. But something didn't sit right with me.

Alistair looked so...normal, all of a sudden. And something in Logan's face told me that he too had doubts. "Kian and Rodney will detain her – and Shasta will detain you. Fair?"

Alistair nodded slowly, reluctantly dropped his sword. Immediately Kian and Rodney were at Rose's side, holding her back. She looked up at me with big, confused eyes. Shasta and Logan held Alistair back.

"She called me a *man*," laughed Alistair. "She'd never called me that before. She didn't think of me that way. We were friends – children together...have you forgotten when we met, Rose? Have you forgotten how old we were?"

"I know how old we were. Children!" Rose insisted. "Alistair, you're being ridiculous. I remember everything."

"How old was I?" Alistair shouted. "Tell me that! And tell me how old you were. Tell me everything – I want to see if you remember!"

"Of course I remember, Alistair," Rose looked like she was about to cry. "We were in the Summer Kingdom. I don't remember our first meeting, of course – we were so young – but I know it must have been when we met for the Apprenticing."

I looked over at Rodney, who looked incredibly concerned. Rodney had told me this story before – after all, Rodney and Alistair had been best friends since they were both fifteen. Rose was only twelve then, about to turn thirteen. And I knew that Rose had met Rodney at her Thirteenth Birthday Celebrations – the Blossoming. All Fey had Blossomings upon turning thirteen –it was deemed the age of the beginnings of adulthood, and they were granted access to the world of magic accordingly. It would have been the day Rose started her Apprenticing. How could she not remember something significant.

"Besides," said Rose, "If you're free of the poison, why did you act like such a complete lunatic about Logan? If the poison didn't make you do that, what did?"

Alistair smiled sadly. "A much more dangerous poison – and a much more common one. Love. I love Rose – I have since I was fifteen years old." He turned a bright red as he spoke – admitting to love in front of me or Kian, liberal Fey who appreciated the power of love was one thing, but many of the other Fey were doubtless more traditional in their worldview, and looked down on any talk of love as unmanly or ill-befitting of a high-ranking Fey. "I have always loved Rose. And when I saw her with another man – I grew jealous. Irrational. Even knowing what I do: the heir to the ruling house of Autumn Springs cannot marry anyone from outside the dukedom. I could never marry her. And I know I must marry a girl from the line. But I can't stop thinking about Rose. Pining after her. Longing for her. Wanting her. When I saw her with Logan just now, I was driven to a frenzy worse than any poison the Sorceress could have injected me with."

"I know that disease well," said Shasta with a wry smile. "We Fey cannot handle it the way humans do – we become crazy." She turned to Rodney who nodded very slightly. "A human disease we Fey have contracted – a disease which drives us mad beyond reason." She was joking, of course, but I could hear the truth in her voice.

"But of course," said Kian, "it isn't always bad. Remember, my sister, that it was Love that helped us to stop the war between Winter and Summer. It was love that brought Feyland together."

"And love that tore us apart," said Shasta. "Love that caused the Dark Hordes to be released..."

"If you do love me, Alistair," Rose pleaded. "Then let me go. Trust in what I say. Stop accusing me..."

"I love Rose," insisted Alistair. "But you are not Rose. I don't know who you are. Some Sorceress, some creature of black magic..."

"How dare you!" Rose cried, her face turning red not with embarrassment but with anger. "Just because you saw me with another man – just *talking* to him, mind you – you assume I can't possibly be the woman you love! Do you trust me so little? Do you have that little faith in me?"

"I have faith in the woman I love," repeated Alistair resolutely.

I stepped forward, not wanting to hazard another fight. I turned to Kian, touching his arm lightly. We communicated through telepathy, and I could see in his eyes that he knew what to do.

"Now Alistair," Kian said. "We're not saying we don't believe you. We know you're the best alchemist in Feyland – if anyone can cure Rose, you can. Not to mention curing Breena. Can you whip up more of that potion – enough to feed both Breena and Rose?"

Alistair nodded silently.

"Then that is what you must do. I will take you to your laboratory, and you can show me what you've been working on. I want to see the genius at work." Kian patted Alistair on the back, soothing him into submission.

"Keep an eye out on the imposter!" Alistair called as Kian led him away. "Don't let her alone! She's the Sorceress, I'm telling you. I warn you – take heed!"

As the two exited, Rodney and Shasta breathed a sigh of relief.

"You don't believe him, do you?" Rose cried in horror.

"Of course not," Rodney said, patting her lightly on the arm. "Don't worry, Sis." But there was something strange about his expression.

Rose looked normal – as normal as Alistair did. Which of them was telling the truth?

I felt a tug on my sleeve and looked up. It was Logan, looking worried.

"Garden?" he whispered. "Now – hurry."

I took his hand and we slipped out of the dining hall.

Chapter 12

❄

Logan's warmth coursed through my body. My blood was warm and sweet and slow – like honey dripping in my veins. The feeling was extraordinary; my whole body shivered with the relief his touch brought me. The cold, the pain – diluted somewhat by the potion – at last vanished.

"It's nice," I whispered as we tiptoed into the garden. Silver-tinted ivy and beautiful red berries surrounded us – the traditional flora of the Winter Court. The air smelled like pine and cinnamon.

"Careful," Logan said, blushing. "Mistletoe." He looked up at the distinct jagged leaves and tiny berries that hung overhead.

"Of course," now it was my turn to blush. My face went scarlet. I couldn't deny it – standing here with Logan felt good, in more ways than one. My mind couldn't help but travel back to that moment on the mountain: seeing his body splayed out on the stones at my feet, feeling my heart beat faster and more passionately than I'd ever thought possible, knowing at that moment that I would rather give my life for his than live another day without him there to share it. No matter how hard I tried to forget, that moment would always exist between us. I looked up into his wide, brown eyes and sighed. "What's going on, Logan? You dragged me out here...is everything okay? Do you know something?"

Logan looked embarrassed. His nose had gone bright pink and he couldn't meet my gaze. "I wasn't entirely honest back there..." he said. "I'm worried. About Rose. That Alistair might be right after all."

"What are you talking about? He's crazy – obviously crazy! Look at the way he went to town on you; why, he nearly killed you!"

"I know, I know," Logan began, "but just hear me out, okay? I think there's something...off about Rose."

"Because she didn't remember when they met?" I looked up. "Okay, that's a little weird, but maybe she was just nervous. You'd be nervous too if the man you loved just accused you of being a secret hell-demon. And you can't deny that Alistair's behavior was just as suspicious – if not, more so..."

"I'm not saying he's behaved like the most stable person in the world," Logan admitted, "but..."

"But?"

"I have to tell you something, Breena. Promise you won't be mad?"

"I promise."

"Back there – in the dining hall. I lied. I didn't want to – only..."

"Only?"

"Only Alistair was so angry and so dangerous and the last thing I wanted to do was get Rose hurt. Or get myself hurt, for that matter. I didn't know how he'd react if I told him the truth. Back then my priority was just getting away."

"So what did happen?"

"When you and Kian were..." Logan flushed and looked away "gone upstairs, I went out into the garden to get some air. I was exhausted. Overwhelmed. And Rose came up to me."

"To console you?"

"At first," Logan said.

"I know things have been hard for you, Logan. Believe me – I get that. And I feel so terrible that I haven't been there for you over the past few days. I know our friendship's suffered because of this whole thing with me and Kian..."

"It isn't easy," Logan admitted. "But we're both trying to be strong. To do the right thing."

"I just want you to know, Logan. That no matter what happens, you can talk to me. Be honest with me. I'll always be there for you as a friend, even if I can't offer you more the way I want to. I know I was...uh...busy when you needed me then" (I turned bright red) "but I can sure promise you that I'll be there for you when you need me. All you have to do is ask." I slipped my hand in his and immediately the surge of warmth warmed us both, making my hair stand on end and causing Logan to jolt upright.

"Did you feel that?" Logan and I both laughed hesitantly, trying to ignore the awkwardness we both felt.

"You felt it too, then," Logan smiled at me.

"I guess Kian was right," I said. "Because you're so hot-blooded, I guess it means you're acting as a sort of heater for me. Keeping me warm and helping to counter the effects of the poison."

"Maybe that's the reason," said Logan vaguely. "Or maybe..." his voice trailed off. "Never mind." He took a step closer to me, wrapping his strong arms around me. My body trembled at his touch. "I guess I'll just have to warm you up, then – I'm glad I can be useful. Usually it's Kian and the other Fey who have magic – and I'm just the chump who watches helplessly. It's nice to be able to be useful for a change."

"You're always useful," I turned to Logan. "Magic or no magic – just being there is enough. Your presence makes me stronger."

Logan shot me a mournful smile. "That's all I want for you," he said, staring into my eyes. His bright, strong gaze was full of love and compassion.

I had to break the connection – I had to break the spell. I was feeling myself grow weak in his presence. "But what about Rose?"

"What?" Logan looked distracted. "Yes – of course...Rose...she came up to me and it started out all...normal. She was asking me how I felt and if I needed anything and if I needed to talk, and..."

"Talk? About what?"

Logan turned away. "Do you even have to ask, Breena?" His voice was full of pain, and I felt guilty for even asking. "Breena, I spent my whole life dreaming of one thing – just one. One vision of how my life could be. And it turned out that I was wrong – so unbelievably wrong. About how things were. About how things would be. I've lost so much these past few years – and maybe I just needed a friend at that moment..."

"You haven't lost..."

"My grandfather." Logan's eyes began to shine with tears. "My wolf clan – so many of them slaughtered during this last battle. And...you." The tears were like diamonds upon his face. "I feel as if I've lost you, Bree."

"Oh, Logan!" I threw my arms around his neck, feeling his warm blood pulse through me as I did so. "You're my best friend in the whole world –

believe me when I say I really do love you. I love you so much. And if things were different...you know I would be with you."

"I know," said Logan, his voice hoarse and his throat cracking. "That's the hardest part. Knowing that you still care for me. If you felt nothing for me it would be different – but knowing that you were so close to choosing me, that I came so close to having you with me every night of my life, waking up next to you every morning..."

"Logan," I cut him off. "We can't talk like that. That's not what I meant. For your sake and mine, you have to move on. I want you to be happy. And you can only be happy when you find a girl that loves you more than anyone else, that wants to be with you forever. Who chooses you."

"Like Rose, you mean?" Logan laughed bitterly. "That's what happened – you see. She started telling me that she wanted me, that she felt something for me that she couldn't control. It started out with just talking and then, I don't know – maybe I was jealous or angry or lonely but all of a sudden we were...I mean, she was..."

"She was what?"

"Kissing me. She just leaned in and kissed me, just like that. And I didn't stop her. I was so surprised, I guessed. But also...confused."

I stared blankly at Logan. I felt exactly the same way. On the one hand, I was glad that Logan had found someone else – even for an instant. On the other hand, deep down – in a part of me I was ashamed of – I felt a little jealous of Rose.

"She was all over me – kissing me on my neck and feeling up my chest and then she was kissing me properly, all over...but it didn't feel right."

"Because of us?"

Logan shook his head. "No. Well, maybe a little. But it was something else. It felt...weird. Almost too much – like she was trying too hard. And that's not like Rose. It didn't...feel like Rose."

"What do you mean?"

"When she started kissing me, it almost felt...this is going to sound awful."

"No, go ahead."

"You know how much I care about you, Breena. And you know that I've never really kissed anyone except you. Except once."

"You had another girlfriend?" I was shocked. Logan and I told each other everything. I'd never known him to keep anything from me before. "When?"

"It was junior year of high school. Listen – you can't judge me, okay? I never told anyone because I was so embarrassed and confused and I was afraid you'd hate me and it didn't mean anything, anyway. At least, it didn't to me."

"Logan, what are you talking about?"

Logan sighed deeply. "Okay, so this one time in junior year, Clariss came up to me and said her dad had been able to score two tickets to this movie premiere for this film I'd really wanted to see – I can't even remember which it was. And she was being really nice about it and I think you were out of town with your mom that weekend and even though I normally hated her, I agreed to go. She was being really friendly – it was the beginning of the school year, and I guess I thought she'd changed over the summer or something. That maybe she was different." He laughed hollowly. "So I gave it a shot. And we went to the movies as friends – or so I thought."

"And what happened?"

"About halfway through the film Clariss turned to me and just started...kissing me. Like, really passionately. And feeling me up. And I was just so...surprised that I let it happen. I didn't say yes. But I didn't say no, either. I was just so surprised that *anyone* was interested in me, let alone Clariss. So this one time, I just...I guess I gave in. Not for long – only for a few seconds. But then I stopped her and ran out of the theater. She followed me but I didn't know what to say. I just kept repeating, "I'm sorry, I don't like you that way." And of course she got furious and told me I'd be sorry. And I never told you because I was afraid you'd be...I don't know. Upset?"

"Don't worry," I said. "I'm not upset – just confused."

"The thing is...something about Rose. It gave me that same feeling. Not just how...you know...how she was doing it, but something deeper. Something magic. Something that just felt wrong."

"You think that was Clariss in Rose's body?"

"I'm not sure," said Logan. "But I think we should find out."

Chapter 13

❄

Logan and I decided that it was best to split up. If we needed to analyze Rose's behavior, I knew, then we needed to get her alone: if Rose was going to try and make a move on Logan, she certainly wasn't going to do it in public.

"Will you be okay?" Logan turned to me as we re-entered the palace. "I know you've been ill...that you're feeling weak. What happens if she corners you?"

I gritted my teeth. I hadn't told Logan about what Clariss had said to me, or about the secret pact she'd tried to make with me. I knew that Clariss wanted me alive – needed me alive – for now. She'd let the poison do its work, but she'd try to convince me to team up with her first. But I didn't answer Logan's question. It would be too complicated to explain – not now... "I can manage," I said, before turning away.

"Bree?" Logan turned to me, a look of love and longing in his eyes.

"What is it?"

"Just – make sure you're careful, okay? I don't want to have to go through losing you again, Breena. I don't think I could deal." He tried to smile but failed. "I've lost a lot. Losing you would just be too much."

"You'll never lose me, Logan," I said, slipping my fingers through his. His warmth was electric; it pulsed through me like fire and I didn't want to let go. Slowly, with considerable effort, I pulled away – our eyes still locking together, our gaze still strong.

I turned away hurriedly. I couldn't let Logan see my weakness – I couldn't afford to *be* weak. Not now. I walked down the corridor towards where Rose was being kept by Rodney and Shasta.

"Are you okay?" I asked as I entered.

"We're just watching Rose," said Shasta. "Making sure she's okay after that horrible shock."

"Alistair's always been my best friend," sighed Rodney. "I can't believe he would do such things, say such things...at least, not when he was in his right mind. It has to be the Sorceress's poison – it *has* to be. Otherwise..."

"He's just gone crazy?" Shasta volunteered darkly. She looked Rose up and down. "You know Alistair – what do you think?"

"It...doesn't seem like him," Rose said. "He's always been so good to me. So kind and..."

"You see!" Rodney cut in. "Don't worry Rose; it's only the poison that's making Alistair act this way. You'll see – once we cure him, he'll be as good as new! And then you can forget all about this."

"I hope so," sniffled Rose. I looked her up and down. Could this innocent, sweet-seeming girl really be an incarnation of the Sorceress?

"Hey, guys?" I turned to Shasta and Rodney. "Can I speak to Rose alone for a second?"

They both looked at each other, curious, before looking at me. "Sure..." Rodney said slowly, rising to his feet.

"We'll just leave you to it," said Shasta, taking hold of Rodney's hand.

When the door had swung shut I turned to face Rose, looking her square in the fact. "How are you feeling, Rose?"

"Fine, I guess," Rose looked down. "I mean – as fine as I can be, given the circumstances."

"I'm sorry you had to see Alistair act like that. I guess the poison must have made him hallucinate..."

"Yeah..." Rose was looking away. "I guess so."

"I mean, all that stuff you said he was saying. About seeing you and Logan kissing – that wasn't true, was it?"

"Of course not!" Rose laughed. "You know how I feel about Alistair! You all do. I'd never hurt him like that...and besides, Logan's obsessed with you, everyone knows that."

I turned red. I didn't want to talk about that. "Be that as it may..." I sighed – but suddenly a light bulb went off in my brain. A plan began to form. I had an idea. "Actually, it isn't true anymore."

"It isn't?"

I sighed loudly – a pretend melodramatic sigh. "Logan's always thought he had feelings for me – but the truth is...he's still pining after someone else. I was always the second-best. The replacement."

"But he always seemed so devoted to you," Rose leaned in. "Always following you around, doing whatever you said..."

"Logan told me that he screwed up with this girl he really liked – ages ago. Apparently they started kissing and he was so embarrassed and nervous that he ran away – he was so afraid, you know, because it was the first time he'd kissed a girl, and he thought he was screwing it up or something..." I laughed. "And he was too nervous to ever talk to her again. He tried to make her jealous by pretending to be in love with me, but it didn't work. Then I guess, over time, those feelings for me became more genuine – he was using me as a rebound, trying to get over this other girl."

Rose's eyes opened wide. They were shining brightly – but a strange, glassy look came over them.

"Who was this girl?"

"That's what I'm worried about," I said. "It's Clariss – the Sorceress. Back in high school we thought she was just a normal girl, but now she's this Sorceress and she's poisoned me, and Logan feels so guilty because he's in love with her, but he can't believe she'd hurt one of his friends..."

"Clariss?" Rose's shock was mingled with a strange, ecstatic joy. A joy I knew only too well.

"Logan loves Clariss," I said. "Always has, always will! And when they kissed out there in the garden – it was electric for him. Overwhelming. It made him realize how stupid he's been all these years – being too shy to approach her again..."

Rose grinned wildly. "Then he *does* love her!"

I turned to Rose. "Or, should I say, loves you?"

Rose's smiled vanished on her face. She glared at me. "I don't know what you're talking about," she snapped.

"Cut the act, Clariss. I know it's you. Logan told me what happened in the garden. Do you really think we don't talk to each other?"

Rose snarled through gritted teeth. Immediately her whole expression changed. The features were still Rose's – but the movement, the spirit – it was all Clariss.

"I'm not Clariss," she said. "Or at least, not totally. I'm merely a shadow, like the ones Alistair saw back in the Wilds of Feyland. I do Clariss' bidding. I am but a part of her many-divided soul."

"What are you doing here? And what have you done with Rose?"

"I just wanted to make sure that you'd kept your promise, Treena," crooned Rose in a cruel voice. "And just as well that I did – because it's obvious to me that you haven't done a thing you said you would do. You're not helping me to win the hearts and minds of the people of Feyland at all. You're just trying to find a cure for the poison yourself – silly fool, don't you know that will never work? You and Alistair both – seeking to make potions! Alistair dares to struggle against the power of *my* book! Who does he think he is? Doesn't he know that it is I who always wins in the end?" She laughed.

"So he wasn't crazy, was he? When he saw you out there with Logan? He saw the truth, didn't he? You were all over Logan, trying to seduce him, trying to make him yours..."

"So what if I did?" Rose snapped. "It's not like *you* want him! You've only ever treated him like a backup plan, a second choice, a last resort. Maybe Logan deserves a woman who is willing to give him everything, instead of only using him when she's bored with her fiancé..."

"How dare you!" I cried, but the words stung. Although I did love Logan, (who wouldn't) I had always loved Kian, too. I couldn't help it because I had always loved Logan as my best friend who became more.

"In any case, Alistair's still crazy. Only this time it's not my fault. It's just that dreadful little sickness that the Fey call love. It messes with their heads. Remember when Shasta tried to kill herself? I know that. I know all about that. Fey feel love more strongly than humans do. So I suppose I did drive Alistair crazy – but it wasn't the poison that did it. He can take all the potion he wants, but *love* can't be cured."

"How long have you been Rose?"

"Only since Alistair took the potion. Once I knew Alistair wasn't going to be my eyes and ears anymore, I had to find...another host."

"And where's Rose?" I cried. "The real one?"

The Sorceress laughed. "Rose is...well, let's just say that she's wherever I want her to be." She shook her long, red hair. "I caught her off guard. When the Enchantress' powers weren't protecting her."

"Tell me where she is!" I cried. "Tell me – or I'll..."

"Or you'll what?" the Sorceress spat.

At that I could resist no longer, drawing my sword from its scabbard. Furious, I slashed at the air, blue and orange flames emerging from my fingers.

But instead of resisting, Rose only cried aloud: "Help! Help! She's killing me!"

"What's going on?" Before I could slay Rose, Kian, Shasta and Rodney rushed in.

"What are you doing?" Kian looked shocked.

I rushed at Rose with my sword. No sooner had the metal collided with her frame than she seemed to erupt in flames – blue and orange – and vanish entirely.

"Have you gone mad?" Immediately, Shasta and Rodney tackled me, pushing me against the wall and pinning me down.

"What the hell do you think you're doing?" Rodney looked furious. "That was my sister!" He raised his sword and pointed at me. "She's infected, too! Just like Alistair!"

"Put that sword down," cried Kian, "It's the poison in Breena that's done this – we need to cure her, not attack her."

"It's not true!" I cried. "Listen, you have to believe me...that's not Rose!"

"It's true!" Logan ran through the doorway. "It's a phantom, an illusion..."

"Do you all have such little faith?" I turned to my friends. "I took some of the potion – my mind is sound. But Rose, on the other hand...It looks like Clariss' plan is only just beginning."

Chapter 14

❄

The others stared at me in confusion. Rodney's eyes were wide with shock and anger: he was staring at me with an unblinking stare. Kian and Shasta too looked overwhelmed. "What just happened?" Shasta looked at me. "Did you just kill Rose?"

"My friends," I turned to them, my voice trembling. "As much as we thought that Alistair was simply under Clariss' diabolical influence – I'm afraid to say that we were wrong. He really was able to cure himself using that potion – and what he saw was real. Or at least, sort of real: it wasn't Rose kissing Logan at all but a phantom. That girl you just saw was a Shadow sent by the Dark Sorceress to spy on you."

"I remember those shadows," Logan said darkly. "When we were in that tavern...Rose and

Alistair were there too...they're powerful. They can take on whatever form your mind fears – or wants – the most."

"She used that trick on us once before," I said. "Now she's trying to fool us again."

Kian looked at me, his blue eyes blazing. "I'm so sorry, my darling," he said. "I was harsh with you just now – I thought you'd gone mad...I didn't trust you..." He walked over, placing his hand lightly on my shoulder. I tried not to wince with the pain of the chill.

"But you thought..."

Kian sighed. "Thought what?"

"For a moment you started to think that I was just like Alistair – that the Dark Sorceress had been able to take over my mind, too."

Kian looked ashamed. "I don't know what to think," he said. "Alistair's acting like his old self again: that much is true. Everything seems remarkably precise, just as he suggested that it would be. He's building up a potion now that may be able to slow the progression of the Freeze both in you and in himself. And then you wouldn't need to rely on Logan for warmth." His voice grew slightly cold. "I still wasn't convinced that Alistair was sane – but he seems to be getting better. Whatever that potion is, it's working on him."

"Well, not totally," Shasta chimed in with a small voice. "He's still suffering from the other thing. Love."

"You know that there's no potion for that, Shasta," Kian sighed. "Alistair isn't used to it – you and I and Rodney, all Fey who have fallen in love have suffered as a result of that temporary madness at one time or another. I only hope that Rose returns his affections so that perhaps his anger and jealousy can subside."

Logan nodded, an inscrutable expression upon his face.

Rodney stepped forward, turning to me. "We have the knights watching Alistair just in case he's still under the influence of the Dark Sorceress," he said, "but now I think we should tell the guards to stand down. As you have said, Breena, Alistair was able to see that Rose wasn't Rose...even when I couldn't see it." He stopped suddenly, catching his voice in his throat. "But if Rose isn't Rose," he said, his voice beginning to tremble, "then where is she?"

"She's alive!" I said quickly, and Rodney seemed to relax a little bit. "I mean, I think she is. The Shadow says that the Dark Sorceress has her where she wants her to be – whatever that means. It's not great news, but it means she's not dead. Whatever power Rose has – I'm guessing Clariss wants to harness it."

"The Dark Sorceress?" Rodney frowned. "That's not good. That's not good at all..."

"What Rose did for me...in the woods..." Logan spoke up suddenly, looking a little bit embarrassed. After all, who could forget Rose's lips against his, the beautiful white light that surrounded them both? "That was some pretty powerful magic right there. Magic that I thought only the Enchantress could perform. Reviving the dead. If Rose has the powers of the Enchantress, maybe the Sorceress has kidnapped her to harness it?"

"I'll call the knights," said Kian brusquely. "We'll send out a search party – search every corner of the kingdom until she's found."

"Wait!" I turned to Kian. "I'm not sure if we'll have any luck at all that way. Physically, I mean. Ever since she arrived, Clariss has been using magic to harm us, to hurt us, to play with our minds. What makes you think she hasn't enchanted parts of Feyland itself to confuse us? We can't just go charging in there without knowing what her plan is? We'll just waste time – I'm sure of it!"

"I think I know where Rose is!" The sound of a man's voice made us all turn around. Alistair was standing before us, his sandy blonde hair falling loosely over his brow, his bright eyes smiling with a clarity that I had not seen in days. My suspicions had been confirmed: Alistair was cured.

"How did you get past the knights?" Rodney looked a bit concerned. "I mean – I'm sorry about, you know, having them stand guard over you and everything, but...they were really there for your own good? In case you hurt someone else – or yourself."

"But you believe me now?"

"We believe you now," Rodney said. "We've seen Rose's true form – she was a Shadow of the Dark Sorceress."

"I'm glad you believe me," said Alistair. "Less glad for Rose. Listen to me - the potion I made is working. I don't feel that darkness in me any longer – I no longer feel the Sorceress's presence within me. I feel...clear, somehow. Like I can think again. Like I'm free. As for those knights – I'm afraid Kian won't want to call them up *just* yet. They're under a sleeping spell that will probably keep them knocked out for another couple of hours. But don't worry – they will be up tomorrow."

Kian and I exchanged glances. Crazy or not, Alistair's power was certainly great: he would go far in our kingdom, we knew. I breathed a silent sigh of relief. Now that Alistair was cured, I no longer felt guilty about refusing Clariss' demands. Plus, if the potion worked on him, there was a good chance it would work on me, too.

"Alistair," I said. "Our first priority is to find Rose. Take me to the Sorceress' Book – I think it might lead us to some answers. We have to find out where Rose is, and if our magic won't help us, we'll have to use some other means."

"Come with me," Alistair bowed low.

Spring Frost: Frost #7

"I'll go with you!" Kian stepped forward, standing next to me.

I turned to him. He looked so kind, so chivalrous, standing there with his blazing blue eyes and his dark hair. I wanted him near me. But I knew that he would never understand Clariss – never know her as I did. I had known her for years, suffered at her hands for years: I couldn't risk dragging Kian into another fight with her, risk losing him as I had almost lost Logan and Alistair. And I couldn't risk letting Kian see what happened if I lost the fight.

"No, Kian," I said. The moment I spoke I felt that what I was saying was true – I felt a sudden wave of power pulsing through my body. "I feel...this feels like something I have to do alone. I think it was meant for me alone to find."

Kian drew me in for a kiss, and I braced myself for the agony of the freeze. But somehow his kiss was less bitter than before. I felt a chill, but I no longer felt the biting torment that had hurt me previously. Even without Logan there to warm me, I felt slightly less frozen than before. How good it was to be able to kiss him again! Maybe Clariss' power was receding...

"Bree," Kian said. "You have to be careful, to take care of yourself. I know you feel that you have to do this alone, but I'm your betrothed. I go wherever you go – I always have and I always will. We're in this together."

"I know," I said, turning away. "But it's my fault that these things are happening now. If it weren't for me, and for how much Clariss hates me, then Rose wouldn't be in danger right now. This battle between me and Clariss – it's personal, Kian. It's one for me to fight alone. She's tossed down the gauntlet: injuring me, hurting the people I love. I'm the one who has to fight her off myself."

"The way you're talking..." Tears were shining in Kian's eyes. "It sounds like you don't think you're coming back."

"It's not like that!" But I knew that, deep down, I wasn't sure. And if I died, I didn't want Kian to see it happen. I didn't want him to suffer. He had already suffered enough on my behalf; I couldn't bear to hurt him more. How could I fight – and risk my life

– knowing how much my loss would hurt him? Something deep within me told me that this fight was to be the hardest one yet. And it was a fight that I would have to brave alone.

"You talk as if you're heading off to some far-off place, and that the chances of your returning..." He wiped the tears from his eyes. "Breena, I know how brave you are. How noble. But now you're Queen of Feyland. You're my betrothed. You have to believe that I will step in and fight for you, no matter where. No matter what. Just remember that I'm behind you. We all are."

"I will," I promised Kian, squeezing his hand and kissing him before departing with Alistair. Out of the corner of my eye I could see Logan frown, sadness spreading across his face.

Poor Logan, I thought to myself. *Poor Kian.* My love seemed to have condemned both men to so much sadness. I loved them both so much – and seeing either one of them unhappy broke my heart. Seeing both of them suffer was almost more than I could bear.

But I had to fight this fight alone.

Chapter 15

❄

"Breena," Alistair said as we rounded the corner, "I'm glad I got you alone. I have something to tell you – but you have to promise you can't tell any of the others. At least, not right now."

"I promise," I said.

We entered Alistair's laboratory. Alistair turned to me. "Listen – after you took the potion from my uncle, he and I spoke. And he told me something I didn't remember – something, apparently, that I'd been enchanted specifically not to remember. There was a time in your childhood when you first had a brush with the Fey – from the Autumn Springs Fey to be precise. You were in your own land, in Gregory. You couldn't have been more than twelve or so. And you found this book – this book that spoke to you. At the time I didn't know much about the book, or about Feyland, so I didn't know the significance of that..."

I thought hard. "I don't remember that," I said.

"That's because my uncle didn't want you to remember. He erased your memory. And Logan's."

"Logan was there?"

"Yes – only those with fey blood could see the book, but you two weren't supposed to see the book until you were ready. So my uncle had me cross over the Crystal River in order to cast a spell – to make you forget. You and Logan both. The book was called the Book of Faeyore. And when my uncle told me...it all started to make sense!"

"The Book of Faeyore?" I looked up in confusion. "I've never heard of it."

"It's the biggest discovery yet," said Alistair. "It means there's another way for us to defeat the Sorceress. You don't have to go into the Sorceress' book as I did, and risk the poison getting worse. You have your own book of magic."

"Faeyore?"

"Yes," said Alistair. "It belongs to you. It's the book owned by the very first Queen of Feyland, passed down from generation to generation. It's filled with ancient prophecies – and my uncle told me that one of the prophecies was about you. A girl from the mortal world destined to become the Queen of Fey. And the book says something else, too. Something I didn't understand until now. That the first Queen of Feyland wasn't entirely Fey either. She was something else – born of a more ancient magic. Like her sisters – the Sorceress and the Enchantress. And it was prophesied that one day she would return in the body of another of her line..."

"Alistair, we have to find Rose. What does all this mean? We can't waste time sitting here talking when Rose is in trouble!"

"It means, Breena, that you could be this third sister. The ancient power of the Sorceress could run in your veins too. It means, you have the power to fight off Clariss..."

"But how? Even if I did...how could I tap into that kind of magic?"

"That's why the book appeared to you even in your human form, Breena. The Book of Faeyore chose you to appear to – yet when you were only living as a human my uncle thought that the knowledge would be too dangerous for one so young. But now you're ready to return to the book. And just as the Sorceress' book appeared to me – so too can the book appear to you. And you can use it to learn the secrets of your magic. And to fight off that poison in you once and for all."

"But where is it?" I was more confused than ever. "How do I find it?"

"That's the thing," said Alistair. "You don't find it. It finds you."

"Where do I start looking?"

"Where do you normally look for books?"

"On a bookshelf."

"Exactly. The Book can hide among many others – just look for it, and you will find it."

"So if I just go to the library and look on a shelf...?"

"Like I said. The book finds you."

"Fine..." I was wary, but I followed Alistair to the library. But to my surprise I found that we were not alone. Logan was already there – an enormous burgundy book in his hands.

"Logan?" I strode over to him. "What are you doing here?"

"This book..." Logan looked down at what he was carrying. "I'm...not sure, actually. It was like something called me here. I don't remember. I just saw this book and felt like I had to..."

"The Book of Faeyore!" Alistair went over to him. "I recognized the markings." He and I exchanged a glance. "But I don't understand. You're a non-magical Fey – how can you even touch the book – let alone find it."

Logan opened the book. The pages turned – by magic, it seemed – and opened about midway through.

"The Wolfstone," Logan read alone. "is connected to the magic of the Ancient Three: the White Magic, the Black Magic, and the Magic of Many Colors, which is the most ancient and powerful of all. It awaits the cooperation of all three kinds of magic before it can restore magic to others. He who holds the Wolfstone is its keeper, and responsible for the three powers and their magic. He must ensure that the White Magic remains good. He must also restore the goodness of the Black Magic, which was once as pure as the White Magic until evil polluted it. He is the bond between the Three – and they will all feel drawn to him...."

"But what's the Wolfstone?" I turned to Logan. "I've never heard of such a thing!"

"I have," said Logan. "Back when I was Delano's prisoner. I started having these nightmares – these visions. And in one vision an ancient Queen came to me – and I dreamed she gave me this stone...only...when I woke up, it was still there!" He pulled the stone from his pocket. It glittered blood-red.

"Then – you're the Keeper of the Wolfstone?" We looked at each other and Logan's eyes grew wide.

"This is what my grandfather meant," Logan said. "When he told me I was destined to have a bond with a Fey woman. Only it's not one woman at all...it's three!"

I caught Logan's eye and blushed, watching as his cheeks too turned crimson red. If what the book said was true, then perhaps the bond I felt with Logan...could it be? I had always assumed that our bond came out of our friendship, out of the time we had spent together in the mortal world, out of the fact that Logan was the only one who understood, like I did, what it was to be caught between two worlds, the Fey and the human. But now I read that our bond was stronger than that; it was fated – it was destined. It reached back through time to the very founding days of magic.

"The bond between the Many-Colored Magic and the Keeper will be one of the most powerful forces in the world," Alistair read out loud. "It sustains Feyland itself. Thus the Keeper of the Books has a responsibility not just to one of the Sisters but to all three. His magic counterbalances the warring magic between the three Sisters; only he can help to achieve balance between the three. He will have no magic himself, but will serve as a vessel of magic for others. His love and loyalty will be the only things that can save Feyland."

I turned bright red. What did this prophecy even mean? I always thought that Kian was my destiny, that he and I shared some magical bond so powerful that nothing could break it. I always

- 163 -

thought that while my feelings for Logan came from the mortal side of myself, magic determined that my feelings for Kian would always be stronger, rooted in the inviolable destiny of magic. But now I wasn't so sure. Was the book telling me that Logan and I were connected in some ancient and magical way that went beyond even my connection with Kian? Certainly, Logan seemed to think so. He was looking at me with shining eyes; I could see something like hope in his gaze. Was he wondering what I was wondering?

I shuddered. I hoped not. I had hurt Logan enough for twenty lifetimes; what he needed now was peace, not more heartbreak. Not more despair. I couldn't risk letting Logan get close to me again, only to tear his hope away once more. No, I had made my decision, I told myself. I loved Kian. I had chosen Kian. This bond...whatever it was...would have to be ignored for the present.

And yet how could I ignore it?

All I knew was that whenever Logan came near me or wrapped his arms around me, I felt an incredible pulsing warmth coursing through my veins, keeping me from Freezing, keeping me safe. When the cold icicles of Winter made my veins turn blue and my skin turn chalky white, it was Logan who brought me back from my pain, who turned me back to normal. He had always been that person to me – the one who brought me back from the brink, who rescued me from my own pain, who reminded me of the girl I used to be and the girl I really was.

But he had been that to Rose and Clariss too. Rose was so shy, so often insecure, yet it was Logan's jovial charm that was capable of bringing her outside herself, of bringing out the confidence and color in her cheeks. Logan had a special bond with Rose – I had already noticed that – whether or not the real Rose tried to kiss him. And Clariss...

After all, Clariss had only started really hating me once she thought that Logan was in love with me. What was it about Logan that had driven Clariss to such murderous rage? Was it love? Was Clariss even capable of love?

No, I couldn't ignore the bond that Logan and I shared. But I'd have to be careful. "So wait a second," I said. "If Logan has a bond with all of the Sisters, then doesn't he have one with Rose, too?"

"That would make sense," said Alistair.

"Then can't Logan use that bond, that energy, to get Rose back?"

"I don't know if I can," said Logan. "I don't even know where she is!"

"But surely you can feel it?" I said. "If you try. It's like me and Kian – magical bonds give you the power of telepathy."

"But you and I don't have that," Logan said sadly. "So why would I have it with Rose?"

"I don't know," I admitted. "But we have to at least try..."

"Before we start looking for Rose," Alistair said. "You should take some of the potion I've made, Breena. It's a stronger version of the one my uncle gave you – it should heal you for longer."

I shook my head. "As long as I'm sick, there's a part of Clariss in me. Right now we can't afford to lose that part. At least, not before we find Rose. I need to keep up this contact with Clariss..."

I looked up at Logan and Alistair. "Because right now I have an idea."

Chapter 16

❄

"Breena, what are you doing?" Alistair looked at me with trepidation. But before he could protest I had already seized the Dark Sorceress' book from his hands.

"What are you doing?" cried Alistair.

"Don't you know how dangerous that is?" Logan cautioned. But I didn't listen to them. I had a plan all my own. If Clariss' darkness connected us – then the more poison I ingested, the closer I'd be to Clariss. The closer I'd be to finding Rose.

As soon as I touched the pages I felt the familiar poison coursing through me, darkness entering my body. Black shadows seemed to rise like inky spindles from the letters of the page; they entered my veins and snaked up and down my body, rivulets of black that filled my body. The pain was agonizing; I didn't care. I was going to find Clariss. I was going to end it, once and for all. I gritted my teeth, feeling the darkness wash over me like a tidal wave.

"Breena, don't!" Logan rushed forth, pushing the book out of my hands. I looked up at him in surprise. He was holding the book, but nothing seemed to be happening to him...the book had no effect on him whatsoever.

"No, I have to!" I ran towards Logan, grabbing the book.

"Breena, please!"

But it was too late. The dust from the books was thick in my nostrils and I could feel the book calling to me, inviting me, beckoning me in...

I was inside the Book.

All around me was shadows. Everything was darkness. Black and grey, white and dark. This wasn't a physical place at all – but rather a magical construction. A palace of shadow and evil. I was floating through it, my wings fanning out behind me. I felt lighter than air, buoyed up and carried through this mysterious place. The ground beneath my feet was not solid, but rather it swirled in smoky whirlpools. Instinctively I knew where I was. This was the depths of Feyland, the recesses of pure evil. The core of Feyland, where the Dark Hordes had once hatched. Where evil begins.

I caught sight of a wan, pale figure in the distance. It was Clariss, clad in a raggedy black lace dress that looked like nothing so much as a spider's web. Her face was pallid – no longer beautiful. There was no kindness behind her harsh, limpid eyes.

"So," she said calmly. "It seems that the poison has finally taken your life at last. It would have been sooner – certainly I hoped it would be sooner. But it looks like you found a potion to stave off the effects. Not for long enough, though, it seems."

I gritted my teeth.

"I'm not dead, Clariss," I said.

Clariss looked surprised, if not confused. "Then what are you doing here, eh? Aren't you supposed to be keeping your promise to me – paving my way to the throne of all Feyland...and to Logan's side."

Just hearing his name on her lips made me wince. "Clariss, that's why I'm here. I wanted to find you. To convince you to join him on the throne. You and he – ruling Feyland together. Isn't that what you want? What you've always wanted? If I leave Logan in charge of Feyland with you I'll have done my duty – and you and he can rule as husband and wife. That is my plan. If you reign alone, the people will be suspicious of you and will hate you. But with Logan by your side, they will trust and love you. Everyone loves Logan in both the Winter and Summer Kingdoms, and even in Autumn Springs. The people listen to him. If you want to rule Feyland, Clariss, you have to go through him. But you have to give Rose back..."

"Rose?" Clariss' eyes narrowed into slits. "Why?"

"Don't worry, Clariss," I said quickly. "It isn't like that. Logan doesn't feel anything for Rose – anything *romantic*, that is. But she's his best friend's sister – and if anything happened to her, he'd never forgive himself. I told you before, but you didn't listen to me. Logan has eyes only for you."

"Come on, Breena," Clariss smiled sadly. "You expect me to swallow that again? I know as well as you do that he's obsessed with you."

"But what if he weren't?"

"What do you mean?"

"Look, Clariss," I sighed. "It doesn't matter to me now. I'm with Kian. I've already made my choice and I'm happy with it. And Logan needs to learn to move on from me, to do without me. Frankly, if he's going to be with someone, it needs to be someone who understands both worlds: the world of Gregory and the world of Feyland. Someone like you. You knew him Beyond the Crystal River; Logan needs that. Logan needs someone who can see both sides of him: human and wolf, mortal and Fey. That person can't be me, Clariss. So why shouldn't it be with you? You have a special connection with him, after all. A magical connection. Don't you feel that? Rose had a silly schoolgirl crush on him – but now she's in love with Alistair and she with her. What Logan feels for you is...strong. Passionate. Maybe he thinks he hates you, but deep down I know how easily hatred can turn into love. Opposites attract, after all. And you two are so beautiful, so glamorous, so right for each other."

Clariss was hanging on my every word, listening intently to each turn of phrase. Her eyes were wide. "Do you really mean that? Do you think I can make him forget about you? Maybe I could use magic," her voice was trembling. "Just a little magic – a little forgetting spell. No, Logan's too proud for that. Too noble. It'd never work on him. And I want him to be sincere...I want a real chance, not some lie."

"Then get me out of the picture, Clariss. Let him forget about me the normal way."

"That's what I was planning on doing!" Clariss spat. "Poisoning you. He couldn't love you when you become a member of the Dark Hordes."

"Do you really think Logan could ever love the woman responsible for my death? If I die, Logan will be in love with my memory – he'll never get over me, least of all fall for the one who killed me. No, you need to let me marry Kian. To live in peace with him. Once Logan sees that I'm serious about Kian, that my decision is final, he'll start to move on. Once he realizes there's no hope. Once I'm a married woman, he'll give up his quest to be with me. I know it."

Clariss looked like she was thinking it over. "He's that honorable?" She looked at me.

"He's the most honorable man in Feyland, Clariss, you know that. Other than Kian of course," I added. "Ever since he was a kid. You know that about him, Clariss. That's why you care for him as much as you do. He's a good man...Logan. He does something to you. He inspires you to be a better person. At least, he inspired me."

Clariss nodded, and then I knew that my plan had worked. Logan's power was in the possibility of redemption – the book had said so. To redeem the Black Magic. He brought out the best in everyone else – in me, in Rose. Why shouldn't he be able to awaken the good in Clariss? His goodness could balance out her evil.

"Now, Clariss," I continued, "You have to come back with me to the Winter Palace. Once Logan sees that you've released me of your own accord he'll realize that you're not as evil as he thought. He'll be impressed. You can start talking to him then. Only...where's Rose?"

Clariss started. "Oh, her," she said. "Rose isn't here. She's too strong – her power was too great. I couldn't drag her all the way down here. I've trapped her elsewhere. Once I return and find that you've not been lying to me about Logan – then I'll let her go. If you marry Kian and I find Logan as pliable as you've said, then I will release her. Now, let's go."

Clariss grabbed my arm. Immediately we were flying again – this time flying through space, leaving behind the strange and nebulous realm we'd just been in and sailing towards the center of Feyland. We flew through the borders of the Winter Forest with its pine trees and mistletoe, flying so quickly that the forest seemed like little more than a blur. In the distance I could see the Winter Palace. As we came closer I could see Kian standing on the balcony, surrounded by knights. Their swords were drawn.

"What's going on?" Clariss hissed. "They look like they knew we were coming."

"I'm fine!" I called out as we approached. "Tell the guards to stand down, Kian."

Clariss released us by the bridge that lay over the moat. The guards were waiting, tensed, poised for battle.

"It's fine," I said. "They won't march without my orders."

Clariss took one hesitant step forward.

Then chaos broke loose. Immediately a knight darted forward, tackling me and forcing me out of the way.

"What the..."

But it was too late. An enormous kelpie was charging straight at Clariss, heading from the palace moat.

"No! Stop! Let her go!" I cried, but the guard was already dragging me inside the palace.

"Traitor," hissed Clariss. "You think you can fight me?" She drew herself up to her full height. "Think again!"

I looked on in shock. There, before my eyes, Clariss was changing shape. She was growing – larger than any human – her skin turning dark and scaly. Her eyes began to glow red. Standing before me was not a woman but a dragon.

"Breena!" Kian rushed up to me, wrapping me in his arms and kissing me passionately. "Logan told me what happened – one of the knights saw you and Clariss in the woods. We know she's taken you prisoner – we had to act fast..."

"Oh, Kian, no! I told her to come here – that she could trust us. We were going to solve this without fighting, without anyone getting hurt."

But that time had passed. The kelpie and the dragon were fighting each other, dealing death-blows with supernatural ferocity. The dragon let loose a furious roar of flame; I screamed as the kelpie transformed instantly into ash, dissolving into thousands of tiny pieces. Out of the corner of my eye I could see Barnaby the centaur – once a dragon-hunter – ride up to face her.

"No!" I shouted, but she had already attacked him, knocking him into the river with a thrust of her spiky tail.

The dragon spoke with a terrifying unearthly wail. "I trusted you – traitorous Breena, and you lied!

You betrayed me! Brought me like a lamb to the slaughter. For that, I will ensure that you never see your beloved Rose again. And I will make all Feyland pay the price of your treachery! This is war!"

And with that, she vanished.

Chapter 17

❄

No sooner had Clariss vanished than the ground began to rumble beneath our feet. As if an earthquake had split apart the bowels of the earth, cracks began to appear in the ground, spreading out like a spider's legs through the earth. I stepped back in shock. "What's going on?" I cried, looking up at Kian. "What did you do?"

A whirl of color passed by out of the corner of my eye. The whirl slowed and I saw that it was Alistair, flying out to meet me, carrying Logan in his arms. The two set foot on the ground beside me. "Hurry, my Queen," cried Alistair. "The Dark Sorceress has begun to unleash the Hordes." Logan was clutching the Book of Faeyore in his hands.

"You have to hurry, Breena," he cried. "Please, Breena, use the book! You're the one destined to share this connection with the Sorceress – you need to use the book to tell you what to do."

I looked at Logan blankly. "But even if I am this third sister," I protested, "how am I supposed to know what to do?"

"Use your magic!" Logan stepped forward. "It's always worked before. Please, Breena, we have to hurry! This is an emergency. Feyland is in danger; I can feel it. The Hordes will rise again if we're not careful."

I shuddered at his words. I too remembered what it was like last time the Hordes had walked the plains of Feyland. I could still see the silver meadows – awash in blood. I could still hear the screams of the dying and of the dead.

"I'll come with you," said Logan. "We have to find Clariss. If I'm supposed to have this connection with her, too – then there's got to be something I can to do to help." He looked confused. "But, Breena – I don't feel anything for Clariss. No connection. No bond. Only anger and hatred. What am I supposed to be feeling?"

I reached out for his hand. Warmth pulsed through me. It felt so good to be near him; the space between us sparked and spilled over with electric power.

"This?" Logan looked up at me with great dark eyes, whispering in a trembling voice. "Because *this* I can understand. This I know I feel – and I know it's magical. I don't feel that for Clariss." I could smell his heat, his animal strength: the smell of pine trees and the woods and wolfish musk that always made me feel so safe. I could not deny this connection, whatever it was. And I knew that whatever magic held us together – it was this magic, and this magic alone, that was capable of defeating Clariss.

"I'll come with you to Clariss," I said. "Maybe the two of us can convince her together to call off the Hordes. She's in love with you, you know. She'll do whatever you say. Maybe if you ask her..."

"How can Clariss be in love with me?" Logan sighed darkly. "She doesn't even know me! She only thinks she loves me because she's jealous of you..."

But I wasn't so sure. I saw the look – so full of desperation and passionate anger – in Clariss' eyes when she spoke of Logan. Whatever Clariss felt, however misguided it was, I knew it was real.

I turned to see Kian dressed in his finest armor, white and silver light shining from his sparkling shield. He approached me, his eyes dark with fear. "I fear we never have a moment's rest, my love," he said. "Breena, once more it seems that we are facing the Darkest Forces of Feyland. Will it never end?" He sighed heavily and I could feel his pain, feel his despair. "Have you taken the potion Alistair made for you? This new batch should cure you for a few weeks more – who knows, it may even destroy the poison altogether. Alistair seems completely cured."

I shook my head. "The poison has allowed me to keep up my connection with Clariss," I said. "It helped me find her through the Book. If I get cured, how are we supposed to find her?" With the Dark Hordes on the loose and Clariss on the run, I couldn't afford to lose that connection.

Kian touched my shoulder lightly and I shivered, feeling the ice. "Let me speak to you in private," he whispered, taking me aside to a secluded recess inside the palace gates. "Listen, Breena, you need this potion and you need it now. There's no use in denying it." Anguish spread across his face like a fever. "Listen to me, Breena. I can't lose you. Even being near you without being able to touch you properly, as it's been the past few days, has been torture for me. It's been days since we last held each other without pain. I can't give you up. Not again."

I wanted to reach out to him, to stroke his face, to take away his pain. His eyes shone brightly with unshed tears, and I wanted to kiss them from his long lashes. I wanted to take him in my arms but I held back, unable to wrap my arms around him as I wanted to, dreading the pain.

"Breena, this has been difficult for me. You know that. Watching you...it's been torture, knowing another man can feel what I only dream of feeling again. Knowing you care for another. But I cannot bear losing you altogether. No matter what it does, no matter what danger it poses to me, I want you to know that I trust you. I accept it. I accept your doubts, your fears, and your desires: all of it."

Spring Frost: Frost #7

"Accept what?" But my voice shook and already I knew what he was about to say.

"Logan," Kian said, wincing at the sound of his name. "I want you to know that I accept it. I know that you chose me – despite whatever Logan feels for you. Or you feel for him. I've been jealous. I've been unfair. I know that now. But I want you to know that I won't let my own irrational fear get in the way of us, Breena. I want you to be with me because you want to be, not because you're afraid to hurt me, or afraid that I won't..." His voice trailed off. "I want to spend my life at your side, Breena. However you want it."

He produced a vial of red-orange liquid from his saddlebag. He pressed it into my hands. "Please, Breena. Take this potion. You need your strength. Feyland needs your strength. We need you to be strong. For Feyland and for us."

I couldn't look him in the face. I wanted so badly to drink that potion, to give into his love, to feel his arms around me once again without pain. I wanted to close my eyes and drink in his beauty along with the medicine, to feel his hands caressing my cheeks. But I knew I could not. Defeating Clariss was more important, even if it meant my life was at stake. And with the Dark Hordes emerging from the depths of Feyland, my life wouldn't last long in any case unless we could bring Clariss down.

"No," I said gently, brushing Kian's hand away as softly as I could. "I can't, you know that. I need you to..."

"Bree!" Kian sighed in frustration, running his fingers through his long dark ebony hair. "Must you always be so stubborn? Listen to me, my darling! I have been selfless for so long. I cared only for duty, for righteousness, for Feyland. But now I need to be selfish. Now is the time for me to let my heart rule instead of my head. I would rather a living wife than a dead hero. I want you around with me – alive – with me by your side. I want to spend the rest of our eternal lives together. I want to be able to hold you and kiss you and be with you in every way as husband and wife. I want you here. Now. With me. When you chose to give up your life for Logan..."

"Please, let's not talk about that..."

"I want you *alive*, Breena. And Logan does too. Both of us would rather die than live without you."

Spring Frost: Frost #7

"Logan's connection with Clariss – it's important. He needs to be alive, Kian. I have to protect him. It says so in the Book of Faeyore: he has a connection with the Sorceress and the Enchantress and the...the third sister. The Magic of Many Colors. Me. And that connection's going to help us find Rose."

"Then let Logan use that connection to find her – and don't worry about your own connection. This poison could kill you!"

"We have to do all we can!" I said. "We can't close off any avenues, not yet."

Kian grabbed me, pulling me close. "Forgive me, Breena," he said sadly, "for what I am about to do. I swore a promise to protect you and to protect Feyland. I won't let you be a martyr. What Feyland needs is you alive, safe, and well." Before I could protest Kian uncorked the vial and forced it into my astonished, opened mouth. I swallowed automatically before I could resist.

Immediately I could feel the effects on the poison. My skin began to warm and turn a glowing light pink. My veins began to pulse silver. I could feel warmth and release wash over me. I started to shake; my whole body felt relaxed, relieved. And as Kian pulled me into his arms, pressing his lips against mine, I felt not the savage pain I expected but pure, unadulterated, pleasure: the joy of being with him once again. Only then did I realize how much I had missed him, how much I loved him. The joy of being with him was overwhelming.

I knew then that something icy within my heart – some evil within me – had vanished. The love for him that I felt now was stronger, deeper, more powerful than it had been before. The Dark Sorceress's hold on me had vanished.

At that moment, I felt the earth shake. We looked up in terror to see the sky itself trembling; it split open like a bolt of fabric, torn straight through. Riding high in the sky was Clariss – still in dragon form – her black scales shining in the light of the twin suns. She breathed fire from her mouth and her eyes were red and filled with cruelty. Three heads emerged from her scaly, spike-lined neck.

And behind her were the Dark Hordes.

Kian and I traded glances. Logan had rushed into the fray already, his sword high in the air. Immediately Kian's and my hands were on our swords.

"So!" A voice filled the air. "You thought you could break our bond, did you?"

"Looks like we didn't have to go find Clariss after all," said Logan. "She found us."

Chapter 18

❄

The war had begun again. Once, I had prayed to never again see violence. The price of war had left me haggard and heartbroken too many times. I had seen my comrades slaughtered, one by one. I had smelled the cloying perfume of silver blood that had filled my nostrils and made me gag. I had fought so many battles on these plains; I had thought that I would never have to fight them again. I closed my eyes, trying to shut out the echoes that burned into my brain: the sounds of the dying, the dead. My friends among them. My enemies. Someone else's friends, family, love. I had done my best for Feyland. I had tried so hard to keep us safe. But here was another enemy, another evil. Clariss was charging forth, the most terrifying army I had ever seen at her back.

At first I thought these were the same Dark Hordes we had seen before: Dark Phoenixes, giants, witches, banshees. But a closer look revealed something else – something more terrifying entirely. The creatures that followed in Clariss' rail were dark, foul-smelling shadows. But they were not pale and formless the way the dead were. Rather, they were solid: too solid. These creatures were made of the very heart and soul of Feyland itself: its earth. I saw wolves made out of rustling leaves; I saw charging Minotaurs that seemed to be carved from the bark of trees. I saw giants whose legs were enormous pillars of moving soil, and – worst of all – I saw skeletons, creatures made from the decaying bones of my fallen friends. The very thought filled my throat with bile. Were these creatures made from the bodies of those I knew or those I had loved? I felt my gorge rise.

Clariss called out to me, her high cackling voice emerging from three heads at once. "You think you can break free from my spell, from my poison, O foolish Breena?" She laughed. "Guess again, my pretty one. This is on you, Breena. This blood is on your hands. Your disobedience to me, Breena, sparked this war. Now observe, so-called Queen of Feyland – although not for very much longer, I must add – these may not be the Dark Hordes you think you know. But they are worse. They come from the very depths of my power." She laughed – a high, long, loud, terrifying laugh. "Let it begin."

She reared up, flying into the air. At this motion the creatures began to charge towards us – thousands and thousands of vile bodies whose stench made me sick to my stomach. They smelled like rot, like decay; they smelled like death.

"Fight!" Kian cried out. "Do not despair, Knights! We will fight for Feyland, for valor, for its honor. Do not fear – we will die bravely, but we will not let these creatures destroy Feyland." My heart leaped in its chest. When Kian spoke – with that deep, booming voice of his – I almost had faith. I almost believed that we had a chance at winning this thing. He was so brave, so strong, my King Kian.

Then the fighting began and my heart sank. No sooner did one knight plunge his sword into the breast of one of the creatures, causing it to explode into the earth, than it rose up again, reassembling from the twigs and leaves and soil that made up the floor of the plain. I gasped as one such re-assembled creature reared up and tore a sword out of its own heart, thrusting it instead deep within the body of its Fey attacker, killing him instantly.

Logan and I traded glances, our stomachs plummeting. These creatures were unkillable.

"Retreat!" Kian called. "Retreat!"

We knew there was no winning this thing – at least, not by physical force. Not even our bravest knights could defeat this kind of magic.

We rushed back inside the palace, fortifying it as best we could.

"Hurry!" shouted Logan. "Get them all inside...we need to block them out. Call all the alchemists, tell them to start researching, start looking for a cure..."

We had never ordered a retreat before – not even in the terrible last days of the last war. But this was different. This magic was different. This was a war about magic. Clariss' magic from the Dark Sorceress was one we could not understand. An ancient magic before the time of the Fey.

Thousands of knights – Winter and Summer – poured through the gates.

"The Hordes are getting through," Kian cried. "We have to close the drawbridge, now!"

"But hundreds of knights are still out there," I protested. "If we leave them out there, they'll die."

"If we let them in," said Logan sadly, "the Hordes will get in – and kill us all. Civilians as well as soldiers."

"It is your decision, Breena," Kian said. "Do we close the drawbridge?"

I took one final look at the hundred knights still fighting, fruitlessly, for their lives. I saw those that could approach the drawbridge, followed closely by the front line of the Hordes, slaying everything in their paths. Kian was right. If even one such creature got into the Palace, it was only a matter of time before we were all doomed.

"Can't they fly in?"

"We have to put up a magical forcefield – nobody can fly in or out of the castle. Otherwise Clariss could get it."

It was the hardest decision I ever made.

I only had a split-second to make it.

"Close the drawbridge," I whispered.

Spring Frost: Frost #7

That night I watched all one hundred knights die in the service of Feyland, perishing one by one against the Dark Hordes. Not a single one of them fell.

Like lambs to the slaughter, I thought bitterly. I wished that I had been among them. They were my men – and they were dying for me – and I did not know how to save them. I did not know how to save Feyland. Alistair and his fellow alchemists ransacked the library, looking for any information, looking for a cure. I read the Book of Faeyore over and over again, searching for an answer. The screams of the dead and the dying outside the window haunted me and Clariss' laughter haunted me. I knew I would not sleep again until either one of us was dead.

It was not only seasonal Fey who died. Logan had called up his wolf pack while I was away with Clariss – it was not until we took a roster of the survivors that I realized just how many people had come to help us fight. Delano was there with his pixies – many of them, I knew, were among the ones who had died outside the palace gates on the first night. My father was there, too – his red beard grown gray.

I waited until nobody was around before rushing into his arms.

"Father," I cried. "They're dead – it's my fault..." He held me as I cried – as quietly as I could. I knew that I could not let even one of my men see me in a moment of weakness. I couldn't even let Logan or Kian see me like this.

"I was never a good king," said my father. "I avoided those tough decisions – I left them to Queen Redleaf. I thought that it meant that I didn't have responsibility for my actions. Today you made the hardest decision any ruler will ever have to make, Breena. And the fact that you made it – it proves that you are the leader I never was." He squeezed my hand. "Those men were soldiers – committed to dying for Feyland. And I'm so proud that in you, at last, they have a ruler worth dying for."

I spent the night looking out over the castle ramparts, counting the bodies of the dead, trying to identify them at a distance to have something to tell their husbands, their wives, their children...

Spring Frost: Frost #7

And then I saw it. One by one, they were stirring. Their dead bodies were vanishing into the earth, being subsumed into it, and then rising again – malformed, rearranged. Their bones became the basis of new skeletons. Their flesh gave birth to newer, more horrible creatures. I swallowed down my vomit.

This had gone on long enough.

"Alistair!" I called. He soon appeared next to me, the Dark Sorceress's book in his hand. I took the book of Faeyore and placed it before him.

"What is it?"

I felt a new anger, a new rage coursing through me. The power of a true leader. The power of a Queen. "I command you!" I cried, placing my hands on the book. Tears were running down my cheeks. "Open! Tell me what I want to know." My rage had gone beyond blue magic and orange magic, beyond Summer and Winter, beyond all divisions, deep into the very heart of things, into the most ancient and atavistic secrets of magic.

"Tell me how to defeat her."

The Book of Faeyore began gleaming with a rainbow light, a light that grew larger and stronger and brighter with each moment. The light began to expand, covering the Sorceress's book within its radius. Alistair dropped it in surprise and jumped backwards, as if burned.

"What's going on?"

We looked down. The Dark Sorceress' book was turning over, shaking, trembling. Its leaves were rustling; its pages were turning of its own accord, sending a cloud of dust into the air.

And then it hit me. The dust had a shape. The tiny grains were taking on a form – a body, a shape, a face...

A face I knew. Rose.

She was standing before me. But this wasn't the Rose I knew. Her hair was long and white; her eyes were whiter still. She shone with a brilliant, pure light.

And she looked mad as hell.

Chapter 19

We stared at Rose in shock. Her body and face were the same as before, but power flowed through her veins – power deeper and more ancient than any I had ever known. Something within me, some deep part of myself, told me the truth: I was in the presence of the full Enchantress at last. She had been present within Rose as an echo – but now her strength had broken through. This was one of the Three.

"How long?" Rose demanded, her voice booming and echoing through the library. "How long has this been going on?" Her voice had weight, authority. I heard in her the power of centuries. Meek, shy, kind Rose had vanished; this new, regal figure had taken her place.

But I was not afraid. This was my sister – one linked to me by magic, if not by blood. "Too long," I said, taking her hand. "Many days, Enchantress."

"So you recognize me," the Enchantress nodded. "Good…" She looked over at Logan. "Come," she said, signaling to him. "Both of you. We must speak."

Logan looked up at me in confusion. "Me?" His mouth dropped open.

"Yes, you. It's the prophecy, Logan. The one that was foretold in the Book of Faeyore. You're part of this too, Logan."

His face told me this wasn't making much sense to him, either.

"Listen, Logan," I said. "I am feeling just what you're feeling – same as you. I'm confused too. Scared. But we have to work through this together. You're part of this just like I am. You have this connection with me, with the Enchantress, with all of us. And now we'll finally find out how."

"There is no time to waste," said the Enchantress, cutting us off brusquely. I marveled at her. Where was Rose – deep down within this body? This wasn't Rose's voice. This wasn't Rose's face. But I knew I had to trust her. I reached out and took her hand; echoing me, Logan did likewise. Immediately we felt the force of magic sear through us. We stood together in a circle, and Logan's touch filled me with that same familiar warmth as he and I linked fingers.

"I cannot defeat the Dark Sorceress alone," said the Enchantress. Her voice shook with the force of her power. "The Dark Sorceress has summoned all the darkness of Feyland to her aid. Her pain, her wrath, her anger are so great. She has taken all the cruel things of Feyland – betrayal, hurt, anger, jealousy, death, decay – and used them to channel her power. It was this wrath that imprisoned me – until together with Breena I was able to break out. It was not until Breena learned to harness her magic, and the magic of the Fey Queens, that I was able to be free. Meanwhile, the Dark Sorceress is charging against Feyland itself: turning the very soil and earth into grotesque murderers."

She turned to me. "You must use that magic, child. Use the magic you have within you. Use it to help me and Logan fight off this darkness before Feyland is consumed with it and becomes a permanent place of Darkness."

Logan nodded. "It's about Feyland," he said.

"It's always about Feyland. It's not about my connection with Breena or Rose or her relationship with Kian or any of it. This is so much bigger than just us. This is between light and dark, good and evil." He sighed. "I've been so blind. Worrying about my feelings when this connection means...so much more."

"You know the power of Feyland," the Enchantress said. "It is a place with magic beyond measure. Those who harbor that magic, that power, will soon burst past the boundaries of the Crystal River, and control not merely this world but the mortal world, and indeed all worlds. Ultimate power, Logan," the Enchantress said. "That is what this is about. That is the true story of Feyland. As Feyland goes, so goes all. You think you can escape to the Land Beyond the Crystal River? You cannot. There is no escape. What happens here ripples through the very fabric of existence."

I flushed. Logan and the Enchantress were right. I'd been letting my personal feelings – my fear of loving Logan, my fear of losing Kian – guide my decisions. I'd been blocking out the truth.

Spring Frost: Frost #7

"Cheer up, Bree," said Logan. "Enough with the guilt trip. You've been blaming Clariss' arrival on yourself long enough. Now you can see. It's not just your fight. It's all of ours. It's something bigger – much bigger – than high school rivalries. Something we can't even begin to comprehend or understand."

"Come now!" said the Enchantress, her voice bending us to submission. "Hold my hand, children, and focus. We need time to build up enough power, enough magic, in order to push those vile creatures back to the abyss from which they came. We must concentrate on destroying them all."

Logan took the Wolfstone from his pocket. Its glow seemed to radiate heat and strength.

"*Remove the darkness,*" the Enchantress began to chant. "*Those who have died in battle, those who have suffered, those who are sick. Let them pass to a place of safety, and comfort. To the Beyond. Let them not be trapped here. Let their darkness not be trapped her. Let them be free.*"

We began to chant with her. Somehow we knew the words; they were in our blood; our instincts told us what to say. A glow began to envelop us, surrounding us with shining magic.

"What's that!" Alistair looked out the window. "They're falling! One of them fell!"

Our magic grew stronger and stronger – so strong that it burned my skin and I had to bite my lip to resist the pain. I had to close my eyes to withstand the brightness of the glow. But Alistair's voice kept me going, kept me strong. "They're dying, Bree! They're dying. The leafy ones are, at least."

I could feel it – feel each death, each release of energy to the beyond. In my mind's eye I could see the leaves scatter and turn into leaves once more; I could feel the bones returning to the earth and disintegrating, giving up their form to create new life and fecundity within. I could see the face of each fallen Fey – flesh instead of skulls – grow translucent and vanish into the great mystery.

"Let the soil itself relinquish its anger, and keep in its place only kindness, only love."

I could feel Clariss' rage, her impotent pain, as the earth began to reject its cruelty, reject the blood that was spilled upon it. The creatures that were made of earth began to disintegrate, too; the blood was cast up over the earth like oil on water.

We were winning. I could feel it – we were winning. Our magic – the three of us, united at last – was working.

And then the roof of the castle crumbled in on itself. A single fire blazed and blasted open the tower like a bomb.

Clariss stood before us, in dragon form – only her beautiful eyes to remind us of the woman she had once been. Her wings flapped and her spikes shone. Out of the corner of my eye I could see the mistletoe in the gardens now charred and broken – the very mistletoe under which Kian and I had kissed months earlier.

"I should have known it was you," snarled Clariss, turning to the Enchantress. "You're behind all of this. I should have guessed. I felt your presence the moment you escaped from my prison. Who had enough magic to let you out? Surely not that stupid young Alistair?" She laughed, a high cackle. "And surely not Breena..." Her gaze fell on me and she stopped, shocked. "What are you doing alive?" She reared up on her claws, ready to shoot fire into my heart.

"Stop!" cried a voice. It was Kian, his armor gleaming, his sword shining bright. His face was filled with passion and strength. "Get out of the way, Bree – go back to what you were doing. It's working! The Hordes are falling! I'll fight her off myself."

Clariss let out a long hiss. "Such love," she scoffed. "Such devotion. Such foolishness. Winter King, you are wasting your time. Why risk your time for a woman who does not love you the way you love her?"

My heart stopped. What did she mean? All my guilt and fear about Logan came rushing to the surface. But I couldn't listen. I had to keep chanting with Logan and the Enchantress.

"What do you mean, witch?"

"The Hordes!" Rodney rushed forth with a jubilant cry. "All except a few. We can fight her off...." He motioned to Clariss. "Rose!" He recognized her with a look of surprise. "Er...right. Rose – are you back?"

The Enchantress sent a jet of shining white light across the room, protecting Kian and Rodney from Clariss' fire.

"Rose is fine," the Enchantress said, "But we haven't got the time to explain. Know that your sister is well. Together we stand. The Wolfstone has helped Breena and I harness our magic. Logan adds to our strength. We have one more spell – and then we shall fell the last of the Hordes."

We resumed our chant. Clariss struggled and cried out, trying in vain to break down the protective shield the Enchantress had created. I could feel the last of Clariss' creatures descend into the soil, bereft of the hatred and anger that made it tick.

The howling of the wind whipped through our ears. And then there was silence. The silence that meant the end of bloodshed, the end of death.

"Do you want to face an eternity of uncertainty, Kian?" Clariss' voice started up again. "You see now the magical connection Breena has with Logan. Stronger even than with you. You and she could not have brought down the Hordes – but Logan and Breena have a connection. She will be forever tied to him. She will forever love him. She loves you because she thinks it is her destiny – but is it? Your touch caused her so much pain – and his so much comfort..."

"That was your Spell, fiend!" Kian shouted at her. "Not her feelings."

"My spell only served to enhance what was already there," said the Sorceress. "You had doubts about her loyalty to you – it affected your love. Ever since the mountainside, when she offered to leave you, to break your heart, to destroy your life...all for the sake of the one she truly loved. For her so-called friend. Let me tell you something, Kian. One doesn't do that for *just a friend.*" Clariss smiled wickedly. "She was driven by passion, mad with love. The same frenzy that has affected you – and to what end? Spending your life with someone who doesn't love you back?"

"Don't listen to her!" I cried. "You know I love you." But Kian's face told a different story. He looked as if he had just been punched in the gut. He looked pale, wan – full of pain. More pain than I had ever seen him in before.

Instantly Clariss transformed from a dragon into the woman I knew – beautiful. Seductive. The kind of girl who could make a man believe anything. Even this.

"Kian, don't listen! She's lying to you."

"My, my," Clariss said. "Such a handsome man you are. You could have your pick of any one of the girls in Feyland. But instead you chose to pine after the one girl who can't truly give up her heart to you." She put her arms around Kian's shoulders. "Didn't you ever wonder what it would be like if you were free. If you didn't feel this pain, this madness? Who in the world has ever caused you as much pain as Breena. When she was engaged to Logan? When she offered to marry him? Who knows what happened when they were under that love spell – if it even *was* a love spell. Who's to say they didn't...that you were the first..."

"It's not true!" My voice was hoarse from the screaming, but the Enchantress pulled me back.

"Do not listen to that shrill voice, my King!" Clariss smiled. "That is your weakness. Always listening to her. Always letting her treat you like dirt – going back between you and Logan, unable to decide, unable to commit. Did you let love consume your powers for this? You're a Fey – not made for this human weakness. Not made for this human masquerading as a Fey Queen."

Tears were running down my face. I wanted to protest, to scream – but what could I say that Kian would believe? I already knew the truth deep down: what Clariss said was right. I had hurt Kian more than anyone else. He had told me once that he felt as if his mother never loved him. That nobody had ever loved him – or would love him. And here I was, the one person who was supposed to love him unconditionally – letting him down. Making him feel abandoned, just as his mother did. Kian's greatest fear – being abandoned. And now the Dark Sorceress had found a way to turn that fear against him.

Logan howled with anger, breaking the circle as he leaped towards Clariss. "Let him be, Clariss! You know you're lying as well as I do. I wish Breena didn't love Kian – but she does. I've accepted it. Kian, you need to believe it too."

I looked up at Logan with surprise. What was he doing?

"Snap out of it! She loves you! She *chose you*

over me. Always has, always will. You couldn't ask for a more devoted love. How many times has she sacrificed herself for you? She gave her life for you. She's been faithful, Kian – even when I haven't deserved your trust as a friend. As a Queen, as a friend, and as a fiancé to you." Logan's face was in anguish. "You don't know how lucky you are...any man would kill to be in your shoes. Fight her!"

"Of course he can afford to be generous," spat Clariss. "He knows he's won. He knows he has Breena's heart in a way you can never have. You should banish him from Feyland, so that he will never again trouble you. Or your fiancé – if you still want her after the way she's treated you."

"I love you!" I cried. "Kian, you must believe that. Surely, you don't believe what Clariss is saying."

"I love you too..." Kian's eyes were dark with pain. "You have no idea how much. But how much can I love you before it's enough – before it's enough for you to remove all doubts?"

"It *is* enough."

"My jealousy, my rage. I feel it boiling up

inside me. I can't control it. And one day it will drive me mad the way Shasta was driven mad. And then I will act irrationally out of this love that has forced its way into the depths of my soul...I will fall into the darkness. I remember how I was when I thought you were engaged to Logan. I was dangerous. I can't take that again. Your love knows no bounds – you can love us both. And you *do* love us both – with so much love. It's one of the reasons I love you – your incredible generous heart. But I can't share you any longer with him."

"I won't abandon you, Kian. I won't leave you. Don't let these insecurities, these doubts, get in the way of what we have...I know about your mother. I know how she made you feel. But I won't make you feel that way."

"You already have!" Kian was crying now. "Everything that's happened since the mountains – your response to my touch, to Logan's. Everything has just emphasized what I thought was Fate is no longer sure."

"That's crazy!" I could feel my heart breaking within my chest. I could see Logan looking at me with such pain, such compassion – seeing his heart break with mine. I wanted him to comfort me; I knew he wanted to comfort me. But I knew that the truth was clear. I couldn't have both men in my life. Not ever. I would have to choose – or lose Kian forever.

Logan snarled at Clariss, transforming into a wolf as he lunged at her. But to my surprise, she countered with a second howl, transforming into a snow-white wolf. "Bet you didn't expect that, did you? But come on, fight me, Logan! Surely you're not against destroying your own kind? After all the Wolves you sacrificed for Breena's sake?"

Logan leaped forward, tearing into Clariss' leg. She yelped, surprised, but fought back, throwing Logan against a wall. The blow of the impact transformed him into a human once again. The Wolfstone slipped from his fingers.

"No!" I cried but it was too late. Clariss already had her hands around it. A black light curled around the stone.

"Looking for this?" She smiled. "Now I can use this stone to control your boyfriend here."

"No you don't!" The Enchantress seemed to fly

forward, grabbing for the stone. The second she touched it, it began to glow with a second, white light.

And then I remembered. *Three Sisters. Three lights.* There was only one way to purge Clariss' evil.

I ran forward, grabbing the stone with my left hand. A rainbow-colored light shone from my fingers.

Three branches of magic. Three kinds of light. Three sisters.

The sound was deafening – a loud, buzzing sound that obliterated all else. The stone began to rise of its own accord, out of our grasp, higher and higher into the sky – a rainbow light spreading out and igniting the heavens.

And then it shattered.

We all fell backwards, overcome by the impact. The world around us was shaking. We were blinded by an enormous golden light.

"The Wolfstone..." Clariss cried. "It's broken!"

"What' s happening?"

"The Wolf Fey magic..." The Enchantress smiled. "It's been released. Logan knew that, didn't you? It's why he let Clariss get her hands on the stone. To give us a chance – all three of us, holding it together. It's what set it off..."

I looked over at Logan. He was shimmering – his body glowing with a straight light.

"Logan?"

And then I saw it. The blood from where he'd hit his head against the wall. Silver blood.

Epilogue

❄

His skin was smoother, softer. His tan was darker. His eyes shone brighter. Everything about Logan shone with power, with Fey magic.

"Are you okay?" I ran over to his side, and as I touched him I felt not the warmth of his Wolf touch but rather something else. Something new. Something strange – something I couldn't fully understand.

"The prophecy," said the Enchantress. "It's what we should have realized all along. The Book of Faeyore foretold this. That only the three sisters could purify the Dark Sorceress."

"Purify?"

I looked over at Clariss. She was staring at us, wide-eyed and confused. "Where am I?" she whispered. "And what am I doing with all these losers from high school?"

Clariss wasn't the most pleasant person in the world, but she certainly wasn't the embodiment of all evil, either. She was – well – Clariss.

And then the Enchantress began to speak with Rose's voice. "Alistair? Alistair – what happened?"

"Rose!" Alistair ran towards her, wrapping his arms around her, the look of joy on his face so profound that it made me want to cry. I looked over at Kian. But his face displayed no such happiness.

I walked up to him, my heart beating fast against my chest. I hadn't seen him look so guarded, so reserved, since our first few days together in Feyland. I touched him lightly with my fingers. The chill between us was completely gone.

He wasn't smiling, but he didn't move away.

"We did it," I said softly, careful. "Kian – are you okay? We did it. We defeated her. We got rid of her evil, of her anger." I tiptoed up and kissed him lightly; he received my kiss without a response. "We did it again. Just like you said we would. We lived through it. It's over. Feyland is safe – at last. And now we can go back to normal. Rule Feyland. Clean up this mess. Plan the wedding."

Kian winced at my words. And then I knew that Clariss' words had struck deep.

"Kian, what is it? What's the matter?" I would not cry – I willed myself not to cry.

"Oh, Breena..." He ran his hands through his lustrous dark hair. "You know what I'm about to say. You know what Clariss said – it wasn't wrong. That distance, that chill..."

"A spell!" I cried. "A curse – nothing more."

"And when you were with Logan? Engaged to him? A spell? And the connection you have with him – a spell, too? When are we going to stop? We blame magic for all that tears us apart. But maybe the problem is us. Whenever you look at him. Whenever you're near him. I still feel it – what you feel for him. What you'll never feel for me."

"I love you! I feel so much for you."

"But I've offered you my whole heart. Undivided. One hundred percent. Can you ever offer me that, Breena? Can you ever love me as single-mindedly as I have loved you?"

Spring Frost: Frost #7

I didn't know how to answer his question. I loved Kian – I knew that. But what I had with Logan...it was a kind of love, too. Not the same kind that I had for Kian. But something I couldn't give up.

"You grew up together," Kian was saying. "You understand things that I just don't – about your whole human world. Your human life."

"What are you saying, Kian?"

He leaned in and kissed me. A kiss that filled me not with joy but with terrible pain – a pain worse than any Freeze. The pain of knowing that this was his way of saying goodbye.

"I need some time, Breena."

"How much time?"

"I don't know." He smiled sadly. "I am immortal, after all. Perhaps forever."

"But I love you. And you love me."

"Is it enough?" Kian looked at me. "Is it really enough?"

"It is for me!"

Kian shook his head. "But it isn't for me, Breena. I love you – but I cannot marry you. You know why."

Kailin Gow

Everything went blurry; everything went black. I couldn't see, couldn't hear, couldn't think. My mind had imploded with the force of his words. And before I knew it I was running – running as fast as I could – down the stairs, through the gate, out of the castle...

As far as I could from the man I loved.

The Fairies of Feyland continues with Logan, Shasta, Rodney, Rose, Kian, and Breena in Book 8 of Kailin Gow's Frost Series™

Enchanted Frost
Fall 2012

PLAYLIST for The Frost Series

War is Over (Kelly Clarkson) http://amzn.to/vfGpxB

The Wolf (Fever Ray) http://amzn.to/uFRey9

The Sound of Winter http://amzn.to/rDe5hX

Winter Song (Sara Bareilles) http://amzn.to/tVr1cX

Killing Pixies (Caelum Bliss) http://amzn.to/tRuTV6

Frost Giant Battle (Patrick Doyle) http://amzn.to/tm8gd8

Frost (Enslaved) http://amzn.to/u7hP3k

Frozen (Within Temptation) http://amzn.to/tn6t0e

Love You Forever http://amzn.to/uXZdUM

My Hero (Foo Fighters) http://amzn.to/vyeosP

Ice Queen (Within Temptation) http://amzn.to/vywWql

Come Home (One Republic) http://amzn.to/sLeK9Y

Breathless (Better Than Ezra) http://amzn.to/urplp4

Kailin Gow

Want to Know More about the *Frost Series*, Author Insight, Author Appearance, Contests and Giveaways?

Join the *Frost Series* Official Facebook Fan Page at:

http://www.facebook.com/theFrostSeries

Talk to Kailin Gow at:

http://kailingow.wordpress.com

and

on Twitter at: @kailingow

Spring Frost: Frost #7

Preview of Upcoming New Series

Loving

Summer

❀

kailin gow

A hot YA edgy contemporary romance

Releases May 2012

Kailin Gow

Prologue

🌿

Rachel Donovan paused at the door to the room her brothers shared, steeling herself for the kind of chaos within. What was it about guys that they couldn't live in any space that wasn't knee deep in unwashed clothes? Okay, so maybe her own room wasn't exactly perfect, but she was a sixteen-year-old girl. And she was meant to be the rebellious one. It was *allowed*.

She pushed open the door to see Nat and Drew still stuffing clothes into their bags for the summer vacation. Nat was a year older than she and Drew were, with short, deep copper hair, an increasingly muscular build, and a good three or four inches in height on either of them. Drew was handsome, built like the athletic star quarterback he was, with jet black hair that would have matched Rachel's except for the purple streaks she'd run through hers, deep green eyes that did match, and those same high cheekbones. Even though they were only fraternal twins, people always commented on the similarities. But the difference was he was tall, almost six feet, two inches, and muscular, while she was average and not muscular.

The room was every bit as bad as she'd thought it would be. Worse, even, because now there were clothes strewn over the two beds while they tried to work out what to take with them, the rejects joining everything else on the floor. Rachel picked her way through it as she headed inside.

"Aren't you two ready to go to Summer's Aunt Sookie's place yet?"

"What's the rush?" Drew asked. Nat just shrugged.

"What's up with you two?" Rachel demanded. "It's like you don't *want* to spend the summer in a Malibu beach house or something. Is the idea of spending days on the beach that bad?"

Drew shoved a few more clothes into the bag, stuffing them down into it hard. "It is when I have to miss football camp for this."

"Like you and the other jocks don't spend all year running into one another anyway," Rachel shot back.

"This is a big deal for me," Drew pointed out.

Rachel snorted. "Like you aren't a shoo-in for some dumb jock football scholarship anyway. A few weeks at

Summer's aunt's place aren't going to hurt. Come on, are *you* really telling me that you'd rather spend the time playing football than on the beach talking to all the girls there?"

"I would if it means you're going to be there in a bathing suit," Drew replied. "There are some sights the world isn't ready for."

Rachel looked around for something to throw at her twin, couldn't find anything suitably heavy looking, and settled for ignoring Drew instead. She turned to Nat. "What about you? What's got you sulking here?"

"I'm not sulking," Nat said. "I'd just rather be here."

"With Chrissy," Drew added from behind Rachel. Nat shot him a dark look.

"Why not?" he demanded. "I've only just hooked up with her, and now I'm supposed to just go off to Malibu?"

Rachel rolled her eyes. "Like you seriously think she won't be here for you when you get back? You two are so into each other it practically makes me want to throw up."

"Isn't that your response to love generally?" Drew asked.

"This from the guy who seems to be making his way around every girl in our class?"

Her brother shrugged. "Can I help it if they all seem to want me?"

That got another eye roll from Rachel. "Arrogant, much?"

Nat stepped in, the way he always seemed to so that they wouldn't end up fighting. It was no fun being a twin with a sensible older brother, sometimes. "Look, Chrissy and I are not in love, guys. Infatuated right now, yes. I mean we went out a few times but that's about it."

"Did you actually want something, Rachel?" Drew asked. "Or are you just here to make sure that we never finish packing?"

Rachel remembered and pulled out her phone, bringing up the photo that Summer had sent over.

"Summer's aunt is going to be busy at her acting school, so Summer is picking us up herself. She sent over a photo so that we wouldn't miss her at the airport. I'm kind of glad she did. She might have been my best friend, but I haven't seen her in, like, forever. I wouldn't have recognized her."

Nat took the phone.

"She's changed a bit," Rachel said, and as her brothers looked at the photo, she watched for the moment when their expressions said they'd finally realized just how much Summer had changed. The slightly awkward thirteen year old in glasses, with braces and puppy fat was gone in the picture she'd sent, to be replaced by a chestnut haired, blue eyed beauty with a willowy body, delicately tanned skin and a perfect smile.

"Whoa," Drew said.

"It's quite a change, isn't it?" Rachel said with a smile of her own, just to let her brothers know that she'd seen their faces. "Honestly, I'm not even sure if I can be friends with someone *that* pretty. I mean, Summer's better looking than the queen bee in our school, so she's probably turned into a total bitch."

"Because all pretty girls are mean girls?" Nat laughed. "Looks like you're going to have to get over the stereotype there, Rachel. Anyway, it isn't even true. Chrissy's beautiful, and she's as sweet as anybody you could ever meet."

Rachel took her phone back from him. "Because you're into her right now. We're see about that in a month." She'd barely gotten her phone back when Drew snatched it from her. "What are you doing?"

"What?" Drew shot back. "I just want to make sure that I recognize her."

"So it has nothing to do with the part where you think she's hot?" Nat asked.

"What if it does?" Drew shrugged. "I've always... I've always thought she was kind of cool."

Rachel gave him a warning look. She knew what her twin brother could be like. "Don't you dare go there," she said. "Summer's one of my best friends. You are not just going to play with her and sleep with her like all the other girls you date. She's off limits, Drew. I mean it."

"You'd better listen," Nat said, with a look that made it clear he wasn't serious. "We wouldn't want to be on Rachel's bad side."

Drew caught his cue neatly. "She has a good side?"

Why was it that her brothers always teamed up on her, Rachel demanded of any part of the universe that was listening? It was meant to be twins who teamed up on the rest of the world, wasn't it?

"I'm serious, Drew," she said. "I don't want Summer getting hurt. Besides, I don't think you're even her type."

"I'm not her type?" Drew said, looking slightly offended. Maybe it was just because he couldn't believe that there was any girl whose type he might not be. "Well, maybe she isn't *my* type. Had you thought of that?"

"She has a pulse, doesn't she?" Nat asked, and was rewarded by Drew throwing one of the t-shirts for Sookie's Acting Academy that Summer had sent over at him.

"He has a point, Drew," Rachel said, moving to sit down on the edge of the bed. "Right now, it seems like you're interested in any pretty girl who looks at you."

"That isn't true," Drew insisted.

Rachel shook her head. "All right then. Any pretty girl who's prepared to sleep with you because you're the star quarterback. You use them and then you leave them, and I don't want Summer hurt like that."

Drew finished shoving clothes into his back and yanked the zipper shut. "Why are you assuming that it's always me?"

"Maybe because it usually is?" Nat suggested. It looked like he'd finished packing too, and he put his bag beside Drew's. There were still plenty of clothes left everywhere. Rachel knew better than to wonder whether they'd do anything about them. "Face it, Drew, you aren't exactly the kind of guy to settle on one girl. How many girlfriends have you had in the last year?"

Drew picked up his bag and grinned the kind of boyish grin that did a lot to explain why he'd worked his way through most of the cheerleading squad. "Plenty. It's kind of hard not to when they're practically throwing themselves at me."

"Well then," Rachel said with heavy sarcasm, "the break will do you good. With all those girls making life so hard for you, this will give you a chance to recover."

Not that it made so much as a dent in Drew's ego. He just shrugged. "I guess it would be kind of good to get away. Then, when I get back, the party starts all over again."

Rachel sighed. There wasn't any point even trying when it came to her twin brother, some days. "Yes, sure. Just finish getting ready, would you?"

"I *am* ready," Drew insisted. He took another look at Rachel's phone, then passed it back to her. "You know, it's going to be good seeing Summer's Aunt Sookie again. *And* that beach house of hers."

"And Summer?" Nat added, obviously trying to stir things up between them.

Drew shrugged. "It's going to be a great vacation any way you look at it."

Rachel headed back to her room, looking for her bag and leaving her brothers behind. Right then, she was kind of thinking that the whole vacation might go a little better if she found a way to abandon them at the airport. It was probably the only way she was going to get any peace, for one thing. But it was too late for that kind of thinking. They were all going, and Drew was right about one thing. It *would* be good to see the old place again.

It would be good to see lots of things. Rachel took another look at the photo Summer had sent her. They'd stayed in touch online, but she hadn't seen her friend face to face since they were both thirteen. Summer was her dearest friend, and she was happy to be seeing her again. She also hoped that Drew would listen to her warnings, because from what she remembered, Summer was fun, and different, and exciting, but also maybe a little too fragile to be treated the way Drew treated girls. She was embarrassed that Drew was the type of walking one-night stand guy their mom had warned her about.

"I hope you know what you're letting yourself in for," Rachel said to the photo, but then shook her head. Summer had always had a crush on Nat, though, ever since she was five years old. No one, no boy had ever been able to shake her out of her crush on Nat, so at least that was a good thing about Drew.

Rachel was looking forward to getting out of the dreary grey San Francisco weather and into sunny Malibu. Aunt Sookie's Malibu pad had always been magical. It was where they can be anyone or anything they wanted. And at this moment, in the Donovans' lives, they wanted to be anywhere other than here.

CPSIA information can be obtained at www.ICGtesting.com
Printed in the USA
LVOW08s1406100716

495760LV00007B/746/P